THE BROTHERHOOD OF BRIMSTONE
GANGSTER SCHOOL

THE BROTHERHOOD OF BRIMSTONE

KATE WISEMAN

A Middle Grade Comic Adventure Story

First published in 2018 by
ZunTold

www.zuntold.com

Cover designed by Isla Bousfield-Donohoe

British Library Cataloguing-in-Publication data
A catalogue record for this book is available from the British Library

ISBN: 978-1-9998633-2-6

Printed and bound in the UK by Jellyfish Solutions

For Mum and Dad,
with love and thanks.

CHAPTER ONE

'Hold that torch still, Charlie,' Milly Dillane whispered, as loudly as she dared. 'I need light to see the numbers on this dial. Safe cracking's hard at the best of times, which this isn't.'

The beam from Charlie's torch cut through the midnight gloom like a miniature prison searchlight.

'Sorry. Gruffles distracted me,' Charlie Partridge muttered, turning his lanky body back and steadying his aim. 'He seems fascinated by that chair. He's got a funny sort of determined look in his eyes. I've seen it before, when he peed against Mum's new sofa about ten minutes after it was delivered. *GRUFFLES!*'

Charlie's dog had taken advantage of his distraction to sneak round a massive desk. Now he was indeed lifting one white, woolly back leg against the chair looming behind it. Charlie's torch clattered to the ground as he launched himself onto his pet, forcing his leg down. 'NOT HERE! Do you want to get us killed? Or worse – sent to Crumley's?'

Gruffles gave a huff and looked as if he was thinking

about it. The dog's leg twitched a bit, but it stayed down. *Even Gruffles is scared of being sent to Crumley's,* Milly thought, with a little shudder.

'Good boy!' Charlie said, causing Milly to lift an ironic eyebrow.

Charlie grabbed his dog's collar and dragged him, stiff-legged and resisting, back to the wall where Milly was perching on a chair. She was battling to open the safe they'd just uncovered, after a long night's search.

Charlie picked up the torch and aimed it at the safe again. He was so much taller than Milly that the chair she was balancing on made them pretty much the same height.

'Remind me – why did we bring Gruffles? He's a liability,' Milly said. She bit the tip of her tongue in concentration as she turned the little dial backwards and forwards. 'Actually, he's worse than that. He's a menace.'

She frowned at Gruffles, who was now looking as if butter wouldn't melt in his mouth, which it definitely would and frequently did when he found himself alone near an open fridge.

'He's here to warn us. If he hears anyone coming, he'll let us know and give us time to get away,' Charlie said.

'If his pong doesn't give us away first.' Gruffles was smellier than the average dog. A lot smellier.

'Drat this safe,' Milly looked up from the dial for a moment. 'This is taking too long. It wasn't this hard in Bank Robbing Club!'

'Want me to have a go?' Charlie asked, peering over her shoulder.

'Don't be offended, but maybe traditional safe cracking's

not your best subject. Remember the last time you tried to blow open a safe? Mr Nightingale wasn't too pleased... Still, the rebuilding's coming on well.'

'He should have thanked me. He's getting a new classroom! The trouble is, it wasn't electronic. Give me a digital safe and I'll have it open before you can say "high visibility display screen".'

Milly couldn't argue with that. Although she'd only known Charlie for a couple of months, after meeting him on their first day at Blaggard's School for Tomorrow's Tyrants, the world's best school for trainee villains, she'd already seen many examples of his wizardry with anything that had an electric current.

'I bet Wolfie would have it open in a microsecond,' Charlie said. 'He's been gone for *days*.'

Wolfie was a flying robot dog with stupendous powers. Milly and Charlie had poached him from Pecunia Badpenny, an unpleasant super-villain with a monobrow and a grudge against the school even bigger than her ego. Wolfie was on holiday at the moment, touring the world as his alter ego, the See-Through Sentinel, righting wrongs as he went.

Milly tucked a strand of straight brown hair behind her ear and leaned her head against the safe. 'Aha! I think I'm getting somewhere...' she edged the dial round an infinitesimal amount.

In the stillness of the room, the click that accompanied the opening safe sounded horribly loud. Milly peered over her shoulder towards the door. She held her breath. No light appeared under it. No ominous footsteps sounded in the still corridor beyond it. Gruffles seemed completely unconcerned.

'Phew,' she breathed.

Charlie craned over her head, looking into the safe. 'It's not there! You were right, Mills.'

It was then that the floor gave way beneath their feet. They tumbled into darkness, landing with undignified thumps a heart-stopping moment later. Charlie's torch flew out of his hand, extinguishing as it hit the ground.

'Ow! What the–?' Charlie exclaimed.

'You OK?' Milly gasped.

Charlie was somewhere nearby, but the blackness was so dense that she wasn't sure where. Even the black and white stripes of his burglar's top, an essential part of the uniform at Blaggard's (along with multi-pocketed black trousers, for carrying all those criminal essentials) were invisible in the murk.

'This wasn't in the blueprints,' Milly said, picking herself up to a crouching position.

A voice snaked towards them out of the darkness.

'That's because it's new. It was only installed a week ago. I'm keeping it secret for a very good reason. So, Milly Dillane. Charlie Partridge. *What in Hades do you think you're doing?*'

CHAPTER TWO

The floor beneath Milly's hands and feet began to vibrate and then to rumble. She had a sensation of upwards movement, back into the thinner darkness above. The floor settled back into its original position.

Now Charlie could locate his torch. He picked it up and flicked it back on, swinging the beam of light in the direction of the voice.

Griselda Martinet, Blaggard's Head Teacher, was standing in front of the door. Her arms were folded and even in the poor light, Milly could see her cold eyes ablaze with anger. She flicked on the lights.

At least she's caught us doing something criminal. That might make her a bit less furious. Ms Martinet knew that Milly and Charlie were secret Dependables – honest citizens with few criminal urges – and she was doing her very best to push them down a less lawful path.

The Head Teacher was pressing the right eye of a poster of a man with dark ringlets and a helpless expression. Milly scanned the writing that surrounded the poster's subject:

WANTED FOR CYBER-FRAUD

VLAD THE EMAILER

IF HE TELLS YOU HE'S LOST

& ASKS TO BORROW YOUR MOBILE

DON'T

LEND IT TO HIM –

HE'LL TAKE OVER YOUR <u>ENTIRE LIFE</u>

IN THREE SECONDS!

The walls of Ms Martinet's office were painted black and plastered with similar mug shots and wanted posters of some very dodgy looking individuals – all ex-Blaggardians who'd gone on to scale the heights of infamy.

Gruffles' ears perked when he saw Ms Martinet. With every appearance of delight he bounced over to her, tail wagging. She wrinkled her nose.

'Thanks for the warning, Gruffles,' Charlie muttered.

Griselda Martinet was wearing elegant camouflage pyjamas. Her face was always pale, but tonight it looked pallid to the point of illness. There were heavy dark smudges under her eyes, and her greying brown hair, usually so neat, was a mess.

She looks exhausted! Milly wondered why she hadn't noticed before.

The Head Teacher threw Gruffles a look of distaste. Dogs were high on her list of dislikes, but she had a good reason for secretly putting up with this one.

'I have to admit I'm torn between pleasure at finding you doing something criminal for once, and anger that you've broken the Golden Rule by directing your law-breaking at *me*, rather than some innocent Dependable citizen of Borage Bagpuize,' Ms Martinet said. 'On the whole, the anger's winning.'

'How did you know we were here?' Milly asked, taking a small step backwards. She'd heard blood-curdling stories about Ms Martinet's temper. There was even meant to be a secret chamber in the school's grounds where Ms Martinet stored the corpses of those she'd frightened to death. Milly didn't believe the rumour but she had a healthy respect for the Head Teacher, especially when there was a pair of decorative manacles and a ball and chain suspended from the wall only feet away. 'Charlie disabled the night-time security, so we didn't set off any alarms,' she added.

Ms Martinet shook her head. 'How many times have I told you – never underestimate your opponent?' Her voice was full of disappointment. 'You know the secret of my upbringing. You should have factored it into your scheme... I sensed your movements, rather than heard them. It wasn't difficult to slip in and activate my new trap.'

She nodded at the photo of Vlad the Emailer. 'You're extremely lucky that I realised it was you before I pressed Vlad's *left* eye. You'd have been obliterated, and in quite an unusual way.' Now there was an expression of manic pride on Ms Martinet's face.

Milly wondered if she was imagining the vertical slits in the Head Teacher's grey eyes. Ms Martinet had recently confided to them that she'd been brought up by cats. With her graceful movements and uncannily sharp senses, she sometimes seemed more feline than human.

'But how did you know it was us? I couldn't see the end of my arm without a torch, and you haven't got one,' Charlie said.

'Cats can see in the dark,' Milly reminded him.

'Doh!' Charlie slapped his forehead. 'We should've...'

'Forgive my cutting your little conversation short,' Ms Martinet said, with heavy sarcasm, 'but I hope you've got an *ab-so-lutely* stunning reason for breaking into my safe. Otherwise you'll shortly be breaking into something else – the nearest first aid kit!' From anyone else, this might be taken as a joke, but the Head Teacher wasn't known for her sense of humour.

Charlie stared at the carpet. Milly knew what that meant – it was up to her to talk them out of the mess they were in. She drew a breath. 'The thing is, we were worried. About Sir Bryon's Brain. Charlie was just kind of – browsing through the school's top security files, and he sort of – accidentally came across a letter to you from the Governors. It sounded as if the Brain's gone missing.'

Milly thought how mad this would sound to a non-Blaggardian. Sir Bryon de Bohun, also known as the Devilish Dandy, was one of the school's most infamous ex-students. There was a portrait of him in Reception that must be deceptive because the man in it looked like he'd rather be preening in front of a mirror than committing dastardly crimes. His badly stuffed body was on display in the Assembly Hall, minus Sir Bryon's Brain – an oddly lumpy but outrageously valuable diamond that had never left Sir Bryon, until his butler killed him with a lethal champagne cork.

Ms Martinet flushed with displeasure. 'Mr Partridge, you're a nuisance. I've just updated the school's security after your last little excursion into my private files. Will nothing *ever* be safe from your prying?'

'Thanks, Miss,' Charlie said, with flush of pride. 'Probably not, if I'm honest. The best thing you could do is to store things the old-fashioned way – on bits of paper in locked filing cabinets.' He grinned at the thought of doing something so antiquated. 'I'm not very good at that kind of crime, but if it's on computer I can get at it. I've never been defeated yet.'

'Like I said, we were worried.' Milly was determined to get to the end of her story, 'Everyone knows the story of the curse. If the Brain leaves Blaggard's, even for a second, the school will immediately collapse in a heap and the Head Teacher will die a horrible death the very same day.'

CHAPTER THREE

The flush on Ms Martinet's face deepened. 'Thanks for reminding me. Who have you told?' she snapped. 'No-one. And we won't. Criminal's dishonour,' Milly swore.

'We're trying to help you,' Charlie piped up at last. Then he seemed to realise that this would only make the Head Teacher angrier. 'In a criminal way, of course,' he added, 'while committing loads of crimes at the same time!' Beneath his mop of unruly hair, he was going almost cross-eyed, trying to look shifty.

Griselda Martinet gave a reluctant nod. 'There's no point denying it,' she sighed. 'The Brain has gone. It must be inside the school grounds. Blaggard's is still standing and I, as you can see, am very much alive. For now.'

Her face darkened. 'If I find out that it's a Blaggardian who's stolen it, I'm going to be angrier than you can imagine. No stealing from other Blaggardians – that's our Golden Rule. And I *will* find out. That's why I've had this pit built – to catch them, if they try it again.'

Milly could understand Ms Martinet's outrage. The Golden Rule had been drummed into her long before she'd started at Blaggard's, via her parents who'd been students there and thought the school was the best thing since lightweight telescopic crowbars.

Charlie was looking puzzled. 'But there's only one Brain, isn't there? Why would they come back?'

'Yes, there's only one Brain, but there may be other rare and precious relics being stored in the school.' Ms Martinet glared at them. 'I only said that there *may be* others. Don't get any ideas!'

This must be Ms Martinet trying to be kind, in her own weird way. Although they did their best to show a flash of villainy now and then, Milly was pretty sure that deep down, Ms Martinet realised that there were boy scouts with more natural villainy than either of them.

Griselda Martinet sighed. 'Well, you've reinforced what the Board of Governors have been telling me. I am *ab-so-lutely* unsuited to the role of Head Teacher. The best thing I can do is resign immediately. That's assuming that I haven't been obliterated in some strange and unusual way first.'

'No!' Milly and Charlie exclaimed.

Ms Martinet raised her eyebrows. 'Why would you care if Blaggard's has a new Head?'

Looking embarrassed, Charlie said: 'The thing is, we *like* you. A bit. Not loads, obviously. But –'

Seeing Ms Martinet's foot beginning to tap, Milly took over. 'And whoever replaced you wouldn't be so understanding. About our struggle to turn truly villainous.

We'd be out of the door in record time.' *And sent to Crumley's, where we'd be lucky to last a day,* she thought but didn't say.

An idea flashed into her brain. 'So really, although it might seem like we're being horribly Dependable, we're actually being really selfish – trying to save our own skins!'

She thought that was a stroke of genius and peeped up through her fringe to see how Griselda Martinet was taking it. The Head Teacher was frowning but that didn't give much away. She nearly always frowned. Or scowled.

'But before we launch our plan, we needed to check that the Brain was actually missing. Which it is,' Milly ended.

Ms Martinet drummed her fingers on her marble desk. 'So, now you've established that – what's this amazing plan of yours?'

Milly hesitated. 'We haven't actually got one. Not yet. But we will have. Soon. Tell you what, Miss. You agree to us helping you and I'll tell you our plan as soon as we come up with it. And keep you informed about our progress. Deal?'

She headed for the door. *Better not give her too long to think about it.*

'I suppose it can't make things any worse,' Miss Martinet said. 'And you *did* manage to defeat Badpenny, so there must be some criminal ingenuity behind those Dependable facades of yours. But I hope you're fast workers. I haven't got long – the Governors have given me till Founders' Day to show them that I've recovered the Brain. That's assuming I'm still alive. And Blaggard's hasn't been reduced to a pile of smoking rubble... Very well, it's a deal.'

Milly had reached the door.

She pulled it open.

'Great. You won't regret it.'

She shoved Charlie and Gruffles through the door and was halfway down the corridor before she said: 'By the way, we can lend you some money, if that's been stolen, too. We've got loads of it. People keep giving it to Wolfie as rewards when he rescues them or returns their stolen stuff. You're welcome to borrow it, if it would help!'

Slamming the door on Ms Martinet's outraged gasp, the girl, the boy and the dog made a run for it.

CHAPTER FOUR

The next day began in the time-honoured fashion, with a quick Assembly. This was Ms Martinet's chance to keep the school updated with any news, and to humiliate anyone who'd annoyed her recently.

As Milly entered the Assembly Hall, placing her hand on one of the fingerprint identification devices before passing the cases of criminal artefacts and the badly stuffed body of Sir Bryon de Bohun, she was aware of an unexpected sense of belonging. *I've only been here for a couple of months, but it feels like home. I know I'll never lose my Dependable ways, but I'm starting to love it here anyway. It's mad and weird and I don't want it to change.*

A sudden loud BANG drew Milly's attention to the reinforced glass holding pen, in which the Tiny Tyrants – the members of Blaggard's brand new nursery school – were caged when they attended Assembly. On these occasions they were steered through the woods from their separate building, constructed on secluded ground just beyond

Blaggard's perimeter wall, by an army of staff wearing riot gear and supplied with shepherds' crooks.

Today the Tiny Tyrants were being relatively well-behaved, although one of them – a three-year-old who was being teased by a face-pulling Year Ten on the other side of the glass – had just his picked up his little plastic chair and hurled it. It bounced off the reinforced glass, landing with a clatter.

Ms Martinet heard the noise and hurried over. She folded her arms and glared at the toddler, who sat down immediately, sucking his thumb and whimpering. Milly smiled. *We've GOT to find a way of keeping Ms Martinet here. She's a genius!*

The Head Teacher returned to her usual place at the centre of the school stage, tapping her foot with ill-concealed impatience as she waited for the students to assemble. The teachers settled into seats at the rear of the stage, in two long rows with their backs to the wall. Behind them, the huge flat screen that had recently been installed in it glowed blankly, highlighting the strange array of teachers.

Milly ran her eye along the rows. There was Edgar Borgia, Teacher of Fabrication, with his wide forehead and frightened blue eyes. Next to him were the dull dress and fierce glare of Jane Vipond, his girlfriend and teacher of Defiance and Discourtesy; then the Forgery teacher, Wilbur Molesworthy, short and stout with velvety black hair and thick glasses.

Not far from Molesworthy was one of Milly's favourite teachers – Marius Babington, stroking his silky beard and probably scheming up the finer details of his next Betrayal lesson. And at the end of the first row, making sure that no one tampered with the fingerprint identification devices, was electronics genius Herman Blight. He was easily Charlie's favourite teacher – the only one who had spotted any criminal potential in him.

The teachers whose specialities were Robbery-related – Gary Nightingale, Hal Steel and Susan Smith (no one believed it was her real name and they weren't too sure about Mr Steel, either) sat together in the right-hand corner of the second row, where they could blend into the shadows. Milly's eyes moved on, fastening on a man who was sitting close behind Herman Blight. She frowned. *Who's that?*

As a Year Seven, Milly was sitting in the row of chairs nearest to the stage, so it was easy to examine the newbie. He was perching on his chair like a little bird that was about to take fright and flutter away. He was short and slender. His skin was a delicate pink, like the inside of a shell. He had feathery eyebrows, beady black eyes and a long, enquiring nose.

He reminds me of – who? I don't know. I could make him into a great cartoon. She made a mental note to add him the list of subjects she wanted to draw in the privacy of her room. Milly had to be careful to keep her love of art to herself. Dependable interests – those with no links to criminality – were banned at Blaggard's.

With the final student seated, Griselda Martinet came straight to the point. 'Good morning, tyrants of tomorrow. First a short, serious warning. I've been told to expect a school inspection this term. You know what that means – Doctor X will be descending on us and poking his nose in everywhere.'

There was a ripple of consternation. Doctor X was the Worldwide Chief Inspector of Felonious Educational Establishments. He was notorious. Everyone had heard of him but no one knew what he looked like. He was held in universal terror and stories abounded of teachers whose lives had been ruined by his blunt Inspection Reports. He was even supposed to have shot one teacher after overhearing him saying that he had applied for a Dependable part-time job in a petting zoo. Dr X was known to be a crack shot with any kind of firearm.

Ms Martinet gave a terse nod. 'Be on your guard. If you see someone you don't know poking around, *start acting criminal immediately!*' Her eyes glittered a warning. 'That's assuming that you aren't doing so already!'

'Now a quick word about Founders' Day. We need some top-notch entertainment to impress your parents and guardians. I'm throwing the responsibility of coming up with some *ab-so-lutely* stupendous ideas onto the House Captains and their Deputies. So, get thinking and let your representatives know what you come up with. This year, it's more important than ever that we come up with something fantastic.'

Milly smiled in anticipation of some fun. They'd recently been appointed joint Deputy House Captains of the brand-new Martinet House, under the leadership of Jet Mannington, a big Year Ten who liked to throw his weight around. It wasn't an easy alliance.

'Let's think of something to really wind Jet up,' she murmured.

'Shouldn't be hard,' Charlie whispered back.

On stage, the Head gave a sharp-toothed smile. 'On to a more cheerful subject. Those among you who are sharp-eyed or sharp-witted – so not you, Blake Thornton!' She glared at a Year Nine, who must have irritated her in some way. The boy dropped his head and started fiddling with the sleeves of his burglar's top, cheeks flaming.

'As I was saying,' the Head Teacher continued, 'the sharp-eyed among you will notice that we have a new member of staff. There he is – looking like a Tiny Tyrant who's wandered into a Sixth Form Intimidation class by mistake.'

Without turning around, she snapped her fingers at the new teacher. He shot off his chair as if he'd been poked with a sharp stick, coming to a halt next to Ms Martinet. She towered over him.

'His name is Gabriel Huggins, but don't hold that against him. We can't all be called Lucifer or Mephistopheles.' Griselda Martinet gave a wintry smile that seemed to be directed at a curly haired Sixth Form thug called Godfrey Goodfellow, whose purpose in life, as far as Milly could make out, was to show how misguided his parents had been when they gave him such a fluffy name.

'He's one of the greatest exponents of Criminal Disguise, especially the famously difficult Lightning Change variety, in the world,' Ms Martinet explained.

The little man went even pinker.

'He'll be starting lessons in Criminal Disguise and Deception with immediate effect. These will replace the old Disguise lessons. All Blaggardians will find that CDD lessons have been built into their timetables,' she said.

She made a little movement as if she was going to give Huggins a pat on the top of his head, but she seemed to decide against it and waved him away instead. He scurried back to his seat.

'This is one of the changes we're making to stay ahead of Crumley's School for Career Criminals. They're introducing some new courses, and there's one on Getting Away With Murder that even I have to admit sounds impressive. They're trying to claw back some of the attention that's been focussed on us since our ghost dog, Humbug, appeared, at the beginning of term.'

Many heads nodded. Humbug had been the attack dog of Sir Bryon de Bohun. There was a portrait of the hound in Blaggard's Reception, together with a little placard claiming eleven confirmed kills for the drooling beast.

In reality the ghost was Gruffles, earning his keep by impersonating the spectral dog. Wolfie sometimes helped him, when he wasn't otherwise engaged. At these times, Wolfie would make himself invisible and fly Gruffles round the woods on his back. Even Milly, who knew the reality of the little scam, found the sight impressive and eerie.

The 'ghost' of Humbug had given the school a real edge over Crumley's School for Career Criminals, their most brutal rivals, and Ms Martinet had milked it by boasting about the ghost dog in the school's prospectus. Crumley's were fuming and were reportedly searching their archives for records of creepy Crumleian animals, so that they could manufacture a four-legged spook of their own.

'The trouble is,' William Proctor had said in his precise voice, over lunch earlier that week, 'Crumleians hate animals.' William's parents had both gone to Crumley's, so Milly was sure he was right.

'They're banned. And hated,' William continued. 'All they've come up with so far is a Victorian hamster, named the Marquis of Bimblethorpe or Bimbles for short, that one of the students smuggled into his room in 1851, among his maiming equipment. It was quickly confiscated – the hamster, not the mallet and cricket bat. I can't imagine that a ghost hamster is going to add much to Crumley's prestige.'

'Oh, I don't know,' Milly had said, momentarily entranced by a vision of a translucent rodent in a swirling cape, trundling after victims on a flying hamster wheel.

She was pulled back to the present by the voice of Ms Martinet saying, 'It's the Year Sevens who will be the first to experience one of Mr Huggins' lessons. Straight after Assembly. Have fun, and if you don't like it, I'm not interested. I wish you a day crammed to the brim with dastardly doings.'

The Head Teacher departed the stage with her customary graceful leap, leaving the school to take in the messages that were now flashing on the big screen:

COMING SOON:
FOUNDERS' DAY
BE THERE, WITH YOUR
PARENTS/CUSTODIANS
OR
BE HOSPITALISED

ACTORS REQUIRED

FOR THE NEXT SCHOOL PRODUCTION:

AN INSPECTOR CALLS

(& LEAVES AGAIN,

MINUS BOTH KNEECAPS)

NB: We are seeking pupils
With <u>ACTING</u> ability

We've got ample offers of
help with the kneecap removal

MISS VIPOND ☺
WILL BE HOLDING AUDITIONS
AFTER LESSONS NEXT WEEK

(DON'T bother if you're easily hurt.
Her feedback will be merciless.)

CHAPTER FIVE

Milly and Charlie had mixed feelings as they approached the new Criminal Disguise and Deception classroom. It had formerly been the Thievery classroom and the province of Nick Lightfinger, who was currently serving a ten-year sentence for betraying Blaggard's. Lightfinger had hated Milly and Charlie, who'd detested him right back.

The Thievery classroom had been extended by knocking down the wall that separated it from a disused room, next door. Blaggardians had been watching the building work for weeks, speculating about its purpose, which was being kept secret.

Every classroom in Blaggard's had a helpful painting on the door, rather than the name of the subject taught inside, to encourage creative thinking. The one on the door of the disused classroom always freaked Charlie out. Even Milly found it a bit creepy. It showed a pair of Blaggardians in early nineteenth century uniform – black and white striped frock coats and multi-pocketed knee breeches – hauling a shrouded body out of a coffin. One of them was clutching a mud-caked spade. The first time he'd passed the painting, Charlie had looked appalled.

'What on Earth...?'

Milly had frowned over the morbid scene for a second. 'Of course – Body Snatching. Foggarty and Spinks, the body snatchers, were Blaggardians, weren't they? I think that Foggarty actually taught the subject here before he got – ' She poked her tongue out of the side of her mouth and cricked her neck to one side.

Charlie had wrinkled his nose and hurried on.

Now, as they passed the room, Milly said: 'They've got rid of that horrible painting. The new one's much more fun.'

The new picture showed Blaggardians in various forms of cunning disguise: a scarecrow, a giant pigeon and even a flowering bush. All had bits of their stripy tops peeping out to emphasise their true identities.

Milly grinned. 'This is going to be interesting. Come on!'

When Lightfinger had been in charge, the room had been as bland and beige as the Thievery teacher himself. Now it was a jumble of colour and chaos. One wall was lined with full-length mirrors, and about half of what used to be the Body Snatching class was now given over to long racks of disguises.

Milly couldn't make out any order in the way these were hanging. There were army uniforms interspersed with sequinned dresses, clown costumes, scout and brownie uniforms, school blazers, chicken suits, plate-armour, muddy sports kit, pinstriped business suits, garish Christmas jumpers, mummy bandages, bear suits, romper suits in sizes to suit everyone from a genuine baby to a seven-foot giant, hand knitted cardigans, crinoline dresses, police uniforms, cowboy outfits – Milly's head was spinning at the jumble of themes and colours.

She selected an old-fashioned striped swimming costume with long legs and held it up to Charlie. 'You'd look great in this!'

Charlie blushed and snatched it from her.

There was also a pile of hats as tall as she was, teetering against a padlocked door. Milly bent down to examine what looked like a furry crocodile lurking on the floor. She tapped Charlie on the shoulder and pointed at it. 'For a second I thought it had escaped from some nightmare zoo, but it's masses of wigs.'

The door opened and a new student hesitated on the threshold. At least, Milly guessed that he was supposed to be a student, because he was dressed in the stripy top and black trousers of the school uniform. But to say that the disguise was less than convincing was putting it kindly. *He looks like someone's dad, wearing that for a bet. Even your average Dependable could make a better job of it,* Milly thought, surprised.

'Hi, guys,' the 'student' said in a falsetto voice. 'I've just started at Blaggard's. My name's Tom. Ms Martinet said to come and join you.' He scurried past the Year Sevens and went to stand towards the back of the room.

All around Milly, students were shaking their heads. 'That's a rubbish disguise – if Huggins wants to pretend to be someone else, he needs to do something about that nose of his!' someone muttered.

'Really, I'm extremely disappointed. If he's a Year Seven, I'm a secret Dependable,' William Proctor said.

The new 'student' looked embarrassed. So did Milly and Charlie, but no one noticed.

The door opened again, revealing a neat old lady wearing a purple cardigan that matched her hair. She took a seat at the desk at the front of the class. She pulled some knitting out of a squashy bag and began fussing over it.

It seemed to take her a while to realise that twenty confused Year Sevens were looking at her. Eventually, she looked up.

'Oh, hello, dears,' she twittered. 'I seem to have knitted a hole!' She held up her knitting for inspection.

No one seemed to know what to say.

After a few awkward seconds, William Proctor cleared his throat. 'Look, I think you might be lost. I assume you're some form of criminal, or you wouldn't have got through Blaggard's security. Perhaps you're someone's granny, here for a surprise visit? But we're waiting for a lesson in Criminal Disguise and Deception, so I'm afraid you'll have to leave immediately.'

Milly rolled her eyes. William Proctor never used one word if he could use a couple of dozen.

The old lady stood up, looking flustered. 'Criminal Disguise and Deception? *Oh dear.* I've never committed a crime in my life! I thought I was in the Jemima Ruddle Retreat for Senile Seniors. Is this a school for *criminals?*

I'll have to tell my son. He's a police inspector.' She started bundling her knitting back into her bag.

There was an appalled silence. William Proctor's freckly cheeks were flaming.

'Cripes. Now we've got a problem. William's given away the school's real identity. The old dear knows that this isn't Constance Bottomley's Academy for the Rural Arts,' Charlie murmured.

Milly nodded, her brain racing. *This could get nasty.*

'Anyone got any good ideas about what to do with her?' a boy called Jake whispered, so that the old woman couldn't hear. 'Maybe we could get a sixth former to – dispose of her, somehow?'

'Oh, I think we could manage that ourselves, between us,' Agatha Quint said. She was a tall girl with a determined chin and a large collection of handcuffs, who Milly didn't trust. But then again she didn't trust most of her schoolmates.

'Let's stick her in a store cupboard while we decide what do with her.' Agatha got up, swinging a pair of glinting handcuffs. She took a step towards her quarry.

Milly darted a look of alarm at Charlie. He shook his head in warning, but she had her limits. 'We're not going to stand by and let this happen,' she whispered, fiercely. 'If they find out we're Dependables, it's too bad.' She stood up too, scraping her chair back.

'Oh look!' the old lady said, suddenly, pointing out of the window. 'Well I'm blessed. That's my Freddie – the one in the blue uniform, in front of those two officers with machine guns. *Freddie! Coo-eee!*' She waved hand frantically.

At the mention of armed police, every head swivelled towards the window.

Just for a moment, before Milly turned away, she thought: *That hand – it's not the hand of an old lady!* But the impulse to join everyone else in checking out potential danger was too strong to give it much thought.

At that moment, a cloud of glittering black mist seemed to billow from the old lady's direction. Every head turned back.

The interloper had disappeared.

Where she had been standing there was a now a life-sized, knitted policeman with googly plastic eyes and knitted pompoms instead of buttons on his tunic. He wore a pointed helmet, which was knitted like the rest of him. *I wonder if his head's that shape too, under his helmet?* Milly hoped not.

Many Blaggardians gasped. A couple gave frightened little sobs.

And then the knitted policeman began to move.

With stiff, conjoined legs, it staggered towards the front row of Year Sevens. Slowly, it raised its arms until they were stretched out in front of its body.

It didn't have hands.

Somewhere behind Milly, a student began crying in earnest – wild, uncontrollable bursts of wailing.

Milly stretched one hand towards Charlie, who was up out of his seat, ready to run.

'Hang on,' she hissed at him. 'I don't know what's going on, but I don't think it's necessarily bad.'

And then, as if to prove her wrong, things got even

worse. From somewhere very close, a siren began shrilling. *Neee-naaaa, neeee-naaaa.* A police car. It sounded as if it was just outside the door. Or even just inside, which was impossible.

At the sound they'd been taught to distrust since babyhood, every Blaggardian head jerked round. Anyone who hadn't already done so leapt to their feet. One boy, a wannabe Stealth specialist called Aidan, had seemingly forgotten all his training and was halfway to the door, knocking over chairs and sending people flying in his desperation to get away.

Another cloud of sparkling smoke erupted just in front of the weird policeman. Heads snapped back towards it.

The knitted figure had gone. And standing in its place was Gabriel Huggins, with a smile of apology on his lips.

'Welcome to Criminal Disguise and Deception,' he said, in a voice that was as gentle as a murderer's sigh of regret. 'I hope I didn't frighten you.'

CHAPTER SIX

For a second there was complete silence in the classroom. Then the laughter began. To Milly, it sounded almost hysterical – the relief of kids who've been terrified and then realise that they're safe, after all.

It's clever, but it's mean. Aiden was losing it altogether! How did Huggins do that? It's not possible to change that quickly. Who was that fake student? And where did he go? Who is it that Huggins reminds me of? Wish I could remember.

Charlie was laughing along with most of the class. 'I've got to learn how to do that!' When he saw Milly's face, he gave her a playful slap on her on back. 'Lighten up, Mills. Don't you think it was funny?'

'No. Not really,' Milly said.

Charlie looked surprised. 'It's not like you to be boring!' For some reason, he threw a quick look behind him.

'And it's not like you to be stupid,' she retorted. For a second the pair glared at each other. They sat down together, but their bodies were angled away.

To hide her upset, Milly made a show of looking around

her, ignoring Charlie. *This is happening a lot recently.* Glancing back, Milly saw that Agatha Quint was sitting directly behind, studiously looking the other way.

When the rest of the Year Sevens had calmed down and taken their seats, the lesson began in earnest.

'I wanted to start with a little demonstration of just how far you can take Applied Disguise and Deception,' Huggins said, in his whispery voice. 'As you can see, the sky's the limit once you get a feel for it. I've had some astonishing successes over the years, disguised as everything from a window box full of tulips to a one-legged Finnish goalkeeper. The key is to completely immerse yourself in the mind of your target. That's what I call the person or thing you want to become. If you can identify with them mentally, you can transform into them physically.'

'I'd love to see him immerse himself in the mind of a window box,' Milly muttered to Charlie, forgetting that they'd just fallen out.

He shot her a quick, relieved grin. 'Me too.'

'Next lesson,' Huggins continued, 'we'll get to work on the basics. I like to build up a disguise from the foundations and work outwards. If I'm aiming to pass myself off as a tramp, I'll start by covering myself in mud and putting on some grotty underwear. For my granny disguise, that you saw a few minutes ago, I start with the lavender perfume and some woolly bloomers. For an animal, it's harder, but I try to stick to their diet for a few days before my transformation–'

'Hope he never has to disguise himself as a dung beetle,' Milly muttered, quick as a flash.

Charlie choked.

'–I also try to move and communicate in the same way as my target,' Huggins finished.

I don't believe it. You can't build up a disguise from the inside in about a second. Milly stuck her hand in the air. 'For the window box, Sir, did you eat worms and refuse to move for a week?' she asked, innocently.

Huggins' feathery eyebrows snapped together. His hand flew up to caress his chin for a moment. Then he gave Milly a superior smile. 'No, dear. That wouldn't be sensible, would it? Bless your heart...'

The class erupted into laughter. Milly stared stonily at the teacher, silently vowing revenge.

'Anyway, let's get on with the lesson,' Huggins breathed.

He turned to the whiteboard and wrote: What's in a name?

'Dependable author, William Shakespeare, writer of all those ridiculous plays where *decency triumphs over felony*, wrote those words, and for once he was right. A suitable name is an essential part of a criminal's disguise. Hades forbid that you should go into any felonious enterprise using *your own name!*' He tittered and the class – or ninety five per cent of it – tittered with him.

He turned round again and wrote two names, FUSTIAN SWAINSBY and BARNABUS DEATH.

'Now, we're going to play a little game. Won't that be fun?' He didn't wait for an answer. 'Let's pretend that you're about to hold the world to ransom. You want to send some threatening messages to world leaders, before issuing your demands. You'll need an alias. Which of these two names would be the best one to instil fear and dread? Hands up for Fustian Swainsby.' Not a single hand was lifted. 'Now hands up for Barnabus De'Ath'.

Nineteen hands shot upwards. At a nudge from Charlie, Milly reluctantly extended her hand, too.

'Lovely,' he whispered. 'Even the short girl with the dark hair got it right this time.'

Milly yawned to show her indifference, but inside she was fuming.

'Here's another scenario. A policeman has stopped you and you need to come up with a non-threatening alias to hide your true identity. I'm sure I don't need to ask which of the two names you'd use under those circumstances, do I?... Good. Even you, little girl?' Milly stared at him. 'We'll take that as a correct answer,' Huggins gave her a condescending smirk.

'I've come up with something that makes it much simpler to choose a suitable alias. I've invented an app, suitable for every mobile phone.' At the mention of an app, Milly saw Charlie's head jerk up. Any form of technology drew Charlie like a pickpocket to a badly fastened rucksack.

'You're going to install it,' Huggins continued. 'It won't take long. You'll find it very useful. In the old days, of course, felons used Naming Dice. The ones made from Orcadian glass are worth a small fortune, now. I had some myself until recently, but I must have lost them when I moved to Borage Bagpuize to take up this job...'

Charlie looked confused. It hadn't taken Milly long to realise that he knew far less about the Felonious World than she did. 'They were made by criminal glassblowers, hiding in caves on the Orkney Islands,' she explained. 'No one's made any for a hundred years and now there's no one alive who can do it.'

Charlie looked intrigued. 'Wouldn't it be great to find some? Although an app's much better, of course.'

'...the problem with Naming Dice, lovely though they are, is that there's a finite number of combinations,' Huggins was saying. 'With my app, the combinations are endless! Everyone please take out your mobiles. Don't bother pretending that you don't have yours with you. I know that they're banned from lessons, but this is Blaggard's!'

When Huggins had handed out the instruction sheets, the Year Sevens set about installing the app. Milly thought about refusing, but curiosity got the better of her. It *did* sound like great fun.

The installation process was easy and in a minute or two it was ready to use. The name of the app appeared first:

INCOGNITO

Milly tapped the logo and it dissolved. A question appeared:

```
What kind of alias are you seeking?

For Dependable, press 1

For Evil, press 2
```

Milly pressed 2 and a new question shimmered onto the screen:

```
How evil do you want to sound?
```

```
For mildly unpleasant, press 1

For decidedly unpleasant, press 2

For downright evil, press 3

For wonderfully, unforgettably evil,
press 4
```

That was easy. Milly pressed 4.

```
For a male alias, press 1

For a female alias, press 2

For a gender-neutral alias, press 3.
```

Milly shrugged and pressed 3. Immediately a long list of names appeared. She scanned through them:

```
Hideon Black

Eldritch Ghoulsworthy

Tartarus Bray...
```

Milly gave a nod of reluctant approval. *Yep, they'd do the job.* She went back a few steps and requested names for a downright evil male.

```
Ruckus Scarabee

Gregor Mortis

Jettison Savage...
```

She heard a snort of laughter from Charlie and turned to see what he'd found.

'Look. I requested disgustingly good names for a Dependable female.' He showed her the suggestions:

```
Gladwina Wigglesworth

Thistledown Blessington

Buttercup Meadows...
```

'Buttercup Meadows. That's priceless!' he grinned.

'I'm glad you're enjoying it,' a voice said. They turned to see Gabriel Huggins beaming at them. 'Have you been able to get the hang of it?' This was aimed at Milly. 'It's not difficult. Even you... ' He left the sentence unfinished but Milly had no doubt about what he meant – *even someone as stupid as you should be able to manage it.*

'Oh, I've managed to work it out,' she said, between gritted teeth.

'Well done. Miss – Dillane, is it? Should I have heard of your parents? Someone said they were infamous, but I can't place them...' Huggins touched his chin and looked as if he was trying to remember. 'The charge for the app will be added to your parents' bills, by the way. I think it's very reasonable, considering how much work I've put into it.'

With a final empty smile he turned away, seemingly oblivious to the glares of hatred that Milly was aiming into the middle of his back.

CHAPTER SEVEN

T hat evening, Charlie was creeping through Blaggard's huge woods. The trees surrounded the rambling building like a living moat, stretching all the way from the infamous Twisted Gates to the playing fields near the rear of the grounds. Beyond these was the Wilderness – a dull wasteland where no one ever bothered to go.

Although it was not fully dark, the woods were eerie – full of unidentifiable noises and tendrils of mist that snaked round Charlie's ankles. A ragged form, too small to be the one Charlie was seeking, fluttered over his head and up into a nearby tree, making him flinch. *It's OK. Just a bat.*

He spotted a ghostly shape, just ahead of him. It dodged through the trees, impossibly fast. Then it swooped high above the treeline, where it raised its head to the moon and gave a blood-chilling howl. 'Wolfie's back, then – making himself invisible and pepping up Gruffles' ghost act,' Charlie murmured to himself.

Hearing a window being slammed, he turned to look at the school building behind him. Already it was too dark to see the school's finer details – the white walls intersected with blackened timbers, the huge, studded front door and the long thatched roof. He could make out the silhouettes of the towering bear statues at either end, though. Charlie found the bears oddly comforting – they contained security cameras and the bears' heads swivelled constantly, searching for intruders.

All along the first and second floors, where the pupils' bedrooms were located, silhouetted figures were standing at their windows, drawn by the eerie cry. One by one they closed their curtains and withdrew into their rooms.

Charlie returned to his quest. He knew better than to call out to Gruffles – all it did was spur the free-spirited dog deeper into the woods, especially when Wolfie was egging him on.

The *crack* of a twig, somewhere off to his left, brought him up short. He froze, straining his ears for more noises. Dragging seconds passed. Just when he'd decided that it was a badger, or a member of Ms Martinet's secret menagerie of cats, he heard a long *swoosh* as the 'ghost dog' swooped.

There was a strange gasp, followed by a sudden jolt of movement, as if someone had launched into a run. Then the woods were full of the sounds of careering and crashing.

Charlie threw himself after them. He'd become pretty adept at tree dodging over the past weeks and soon he'd gained enough ground to witness a dramatic tableau. The first thing he saw was a figure, arms outstretched in front of it as it ran. It was draped in a dark hooded robe. The heavy garment hampered the wearer's movements, and the figure was constantly getting its legs caught up in the robe's folds. Again and again it stumbled, forcing Charlie to duck behind the nearest tree to avoid being seen. Sometimes the figure managed to right itself. Sometimes it fell to the ground and had to scramble up to resume its escape.

The 'ghost dog' was swooping around behind it. Gruffles and Wolfie were obviously having a wonderful time. They would come within biting distance of their victim, with Gruffles snarling and showing his teeth, which were glowing green. For a moment this flummoxed Charlie, until he realised that Wolfie must have done something to them, to make the 'ghost dog' even more frightening. At the last moment they would drop back and allow their prey to surge away. But not for long.

The robed figure seemed to know where it was heading. It was weaving towards the deepest part of the woods. Charlie followed, nose wrinkled as he became aware of a smell so hideous that it seemed to drape itself over everything like a stinking blanket.

A squat building lurked ahead, flanked by dense evergreen trees. *He can't be.* Charlie thought. *Doesn't he know what that is? He's mad!* The robed figure was heading for a metal door bearing a rusted sign:

WARNING – **KILLER SEWAGE**

THIS HAS NOT BEEN EMPTIED SINCE 1948

APPROACH AT YOUR OWN RISK

Every Blaggardian knew better than to go anywhere near the sewage container. There were dozens of stories about it – many of them featuring hapless students who'd dared to go inside and were never seen again. There was even one about how Sir Bryon de Bohun had drowned a rival for title 'Britain's Best-dressed Baddie, 1820' in it, although William Proctor had dampened the atmosphere of ghoulish glee by pointing out that at that time, effluent would have simply been dumped into the nearest river.

Charlie's favourite story told of the little building receiving a direct hit from a bomb dropped by a Zeppelin during the First World War. The explosion had driven the vile contents so high into the air that they'd landed all over the slow-moving dirigible, which had melted like a corpse in acid. As a result of this, Blaggard's 'cover' school, Constance Bottomley's Academy for the Rural Arts, had been awarded a medal by King George V, who'd caused endless trouble by trying to visit the school in person to shake everyone's hand.

In the end, the Head Teacher had been forced to come up with a Fabrication, telling the King that everyone at the school had gone down with Plague. His Majesty had responded by cancelling his visit and sending a large consignment of spot cream to help in the students' recovery. It had been stored in the Chemistry Department for use in Improvised Weaponry classes. There was still a lot of it left, festering in dusty jars.

'One day, we're sure to find a use for it,' William Proctor had observed. 'I'm convinced that it contains all manner of lovely toxic ingredients. I took a peek at it the other day. It's gone luminous green!'

The robed figure was crashing through the trees towards the sewage processor. *He's not slowing down. He'll smash straight into the door,* Charlie thought, wincing in anticipation. Fleetingly he considered yelling at the figure, telling it to stop while it still could. But something was telling him to keep his mouth shut.

The figure was just metres from the door now and still running at full pelt, with the flying fiend snapping at its heels.

Just when Charlie thought that there was no way that the figure could avoid slamming into the door, it bawled out a single word: *'BRIMSTONE'.* Charlie noticed that the voice had an unearthly quality. The door swung open and the figure vanished inside, closely followed by the 'ghost dog'.

The door was closing.

Charlie had a decision to make. He could go in before it slammed shut, or wait until he'd had a chance to weigh up his options. He'd heard what must be the password, so he'd be able to get the door open. But he might alert the robed figure, and his instincts were telling him that he didn't want to do that.

What would Milly do? I wish she wasn't in detention for doing her Forgery homework. She only did it to annoy Molesworthy – she made sure she got it all wrong... No question about what she'd do. She'd go and get Gruffles and Wolfie out.

He started forward. Half a second too late. The door was

rumbling to a close. Already the gap was too narrow for him to slip through. Desperately, he glanced around him for something to jam into the diminishing space.

Lying to one side was a rusting metal shard, about the length of Charlie's arm from his elbow to his fingertips. He wondered if it was a remnant of the melted Zeppelin. He snatched it up and shoved it into the gap. The metal buckled under the force of the closing door, leaving just the tiniest slit of blackness around its edge.

CHAPTER EIGHT

Charlie examined the miniscule gap despondently. A mouse couldn't squeeze through it, let alone a tall boy with a generous amount of hair. He bent his head close to the gap and strained his ears. Silence. *Maybe that's a good thing?*

He wondered what to do.

Most of the length of rusty metal was on his side of the door. He decided to try to use it as a lever, and crossed his fingers that it didn't snap under the strain.

Holding the bar in front of him like a rower with an oar, he pulled back on it. The metal buckled some more. He stopped pulling, adjusted his grip, set his shoulders and heaved with all his strength. The sharp edges of the metal dug into his hands. He felt warm sweat trickling down his back, which had been chilled by the night air. Then, slowly and smoothly, the door opened. He slipped inside.

Immediately, he had to stop again.

He was in a space as black as a villain's heart and he could see absolutely nothing. He had no idea if he was in a vast cavern or a broom cupboard. *Better hang on till my eyes adjust. For all I know there's a bottomless well just in front of me.* As he waited, his ears were straining for some indication that Gruffles, or Wolfie, or the robed figure, were somewhere nearby.

There were a couple of things that struck him as odd. The first was that it wasn't as cold as he'd expected. Subconsciously, he'd expected the temperature to drop as it had when he and Milly had taken their first steps into the secret tunnels that ran around most of the school. He wasn't exactly an expert on sewage storage, but it seemed to make sense to keep it cool to minimise the stink. But in here it was pleasantly warm.

The other odd thing was connected to the pong. It had disappeared, just like that. On the other side of the door, it was so strong it seemed to delve into your skull. But a few steps through the door and the air was completely clear. *Weird!*

Sudden bright light hurt Charlie's eyes. For the first time he could see where he was, and for a second he was rooted to the spot. Then he came to his senses and glanced around, looking for the robed figure. It was nowhere to be seen. He checked again, this time for surveillance devices that could betray his presence. It seemed that he was in luck – there were none. Or at least, none that he could see.

Somewhere out of sight, he could hear sounds of movement. *I wonder if that's the weirdo in the robe. Where are Wolfie and Gruffles?*

Much closer by, he heard a faint but jaunty PERP. *Aha!*

That's Wolfie. If he's perping, he's safe. And if he's safe, so is Gruffles.

Satisfied that Wolfie and Gruffles were in no immediate danger, Charlie assessed his surroundings. There was no sign of a seeping sewage tank. Actually there was no tank of any description. Or sewage, for that matter.

He was in a long room with a gently curving roof and walls, a bit like a long brick igloo. It stretched back some distance before veering round to the right, in a boomerang shape. Glowing electric lights were attached to the walls at intervals. They illuminated stacks of wooden crates, a supply of giant aerosol cans the size of fire extinguishers, a huge, old-fashioned safe and, for some reason, a life-sized reproduction of Charlie's least favourite of all Blaggard's relics – the badly stuffed body of Sir Bryon de Bohun. It was accurate down to the tiniest detail – the expression of pained surprise on the face, the jaw with its exposed bone, the wonky eyes. *This is getting weirder by the second!*

There was a platform in the middle of the room, about as high as Charlie's waist and the size of a big door. A heavy black blanket was draped over it, sweeping down to the floor.

Charlie spared a second or two to look at the cloth. It was obviously old, and it was embroidered all over with pistols and swords and skulls and little bottles and – what were these strange things that looked like low tables with a single upright wooden pole in the middle of each one? He squinted at them for a second more before enlightenment hit him. *Little sets of gallows – charming!*

Around the corner, Charlie heard strange, alien voices. The robed figure had joined others, who must have been already waiting in this strange place. The voices were getting louder. *I'd better hide!*

Charlie folded his lanky body and ducked beneath the black-shrouded platform.

And found that he wasn't alone.

Gruffles and Wolfie were squashed under there, too. The robot dog had settled in one corner and was directing its ear and tail probes towards the voices. When it saw Charlie its eyes glowed a joyful yellow for a moment and it gave a tiny, welcoming *perp!*

'Shhh!' Charlie hissed the warning. He turned to glower at Gruffles, who was looking guilty and excited at the same time.

There was no time for further communication, because the owners of the alien voices seemed to have come to a halt just outside their hideaway.

'Sorry I'm late. I had some detentions,' said one strange voice. 'And I had to deal with that wretched ghost hound.' It was still breathing heavily, as if it had been taking strenuous exercise.

That's the one Gruffles chased. And then Charlie had an idea. *Detention? A teacher then! Milly's in detention. Could it be Mr Molesworthy? How many other teachers are holding detentions tonight?*

'It's getting harder and harder to get to meetings. It's always on the prowl,' the voice continued.

'We should do something about it,' another weird voice replied. 'We were here first. The woods are *ours*. Always have been. Where did the ghost dog come from anyway? Maybe we can exorcise it? What do you think, Brother Inferior?'

'Exercise it, Brother Anterior? Don't you think it gets enough exercise, chasing us around?' Voice One replied, wearily.

'ExORcise, not exercise, you feeble excuse for a villain! No wonder you're the Brother Inferior. I've had handcuffs with more criminal brainpower than you!' Voice Two sounded like an exasperated Martian.

'The sooner we find a way to get rid of that ghost, the better,' offered a third alien voice. This one's sentences were punctuated with a strange whining *w-h-e-e-b* noise. 'It's hard to get into the right mind set for horrific *w-h-e-e-b* ceremonies when you've just been chased around like a chicken with a fox after it.'

'Speaking of chickens, we'd better get ready for the ceremony,' Voice Two said. 'The Brother Superior will be here any second, and we don't want to keep him waiting.'

'No! He's nasty when he's angry. Go and get the *w-h-e-e-b* chicken, Brother Inferior.'

'Why am I always the one to get the chicken?' This was Voice One again. 'I'm not suggesting *you* should do such a menial task, Brother Anterior, but the Brother Superior could get that apprentice of his to help out. He never does anything useful...'

The voice tailed off as its owner walked away. The footsteps of the other two receded into the distance. Charlie threw a look of warning at his companions and put one finger to his lips. Wolfie's eyes flashed yellow for a second to show that he understood. Gruffles just wagged his tail, which could mean pretty well anything.

Charlie stared ahead of him, trying to make sense of what he'd heard. There was some kind of weird club meeting there. Judging from their complaints about the ghost dog in *their* woods, they had been meeting for a long time. They had aliases and they were using something to disguise their voices. They were led by someone called the Brother Superior who scared the others, and they were going to have some kind of ceremony involving a chicken. *Don't like the sound of that,* Charlie thought.

Had he learned anything else? Yes. *They must be Blaggardians – they seem to know the grounds really well, and how else could they get inside the Twisted Gates and all the security? And at least one of them is a teacher.*

There was no time to ponder more. The door to the den was opening again.

CHAPTER NINE

Crouching beneath the table and peering beneath the hem of the black blanket, Charlie saw two sets of feet approaching him, both clad in black trainers. Although Charlie couldn't see higher than the figures' knees, he saw that there were long robes swishing around their legs – one black, the other grey.

The black robe was a little different to the others. It was embroidered with the same motifs as the blanket that lay on the table, but on the robe the gallows weren't empty. There were tiny men swinging from them. He wrinkled his nose in disgust.

'We made it! No ghost dog today,' a new voice said. This one was disguised too, but differently to the others. *They* all sounded like cartoon aliens. *This* voice was rumbly and too low to be natural. *If a bear could talk, it would sound like that.*

'That's assuming it *is* a ghost dog. I've got my suspicions. I thought I saw it peeing against a tree the other day,' the deep voice continued.

Charlie rolled his eyes. The sets of feet moved out of his line of sight and followed the others around the corner.

'They'd better have sorted out the chicken issue,' the gruff voice said. 'The last ceremony was more like a third-rate comedy than a sacred rite. Sir Bryon would be turning in his grave, if he had one.'

'Don't worry, master,' another voice replied. 'The Brother Inferior was saying that he's come up with a much better standard of sacrifice. No more frozen chickens for the Brotherhood of Brimstone!'

'I'm relieved to hear that, Maggot. I assume you've got the knife?'

The voices moved beyond earshot.

Charlie was staring at Gruffles, horrified. 'They're going to sacrifice a chicken. That's *horrible*,' Charlie whispered.

He crawled out from under the table. Wolfie emerged, too, followed by Gruffles. Wolfie did a little shimmy, which Gruffles seemed to understand was an invitation to climb onto his back. Charlie tiptoed towards the back of the room, followed by both dogs.

He peered around the corner.

The five robed figures were hunched in a circle, examining something that the shortest Brother – the Brother Inferior – was pulling from a large wooden crate. Charlie couldn't see it clearly, but it looked lumpy and bedraggled. It gave a strangled wheeze. *The chicken! It sounds really ill!* His initial impulse was to launch himself onto the group and grab the unfortunate bird, but he restrained himself. There were too many of them.

The Brother in the embroidered robe took the creature

gingerly by its neck and subjected it to detailed examination. It lay utterly still in his gloved hands. *Maybe it's already dead?* Charlie wondered.

'Congratulations, Brother Inferior,' the deep-voiced Brother rumbled. 'It's the worst yet. Where did you get it from?'

He turned towards Charlie, giving him a clear view of the creature in his hands. It was luminous yellow and its neck was long and thin as a sodden sock. Its skinny red legs dangled limply over the Brother Superior's hand. He poked its tummy. It gave a strangled *EEEK.*

It's rubber! Charlie realised.

'It sounds like a whoopee cushion,' the tallest of the Brothers – Anterior? – said. His robe was dark green, like poison bottles.

The Brother Inferior took the rubber chicken and cradled it against his brown robe. 'It's impossible to get live chickens any more,' he moaned. 'Too many rules and regulations.'

'*Rules and regulations?* We're an evil sect, dedicated to completing Pecunia Badpenny's mission and bringing misery to Dependables everywhere.'

Charlie frowned into Wolfie's eyes. *Completing Badpenny's mission? Her mission to destroy Blaggard's?*

'What do you think you should do with rules?' Superior's voice was rich with sarcasm.

'Ignore them,' Inferior said. 'But–'

'No buts,' Superior interrupted. He gave a sigh. 'So, where did you acquire this outstanding specimen?'

'Crimbay,' Inferior said. 'There was a special offer for bulk buys...'

'–BULK buys? *W-h-e-e-b!* How many have we got to get through?' This was the other Brother – Brother Posterior – whose robe was blackish red.

In a tiny voice, the small Brother said: 'A hundred or so... But I've had a great idea to make them more realistic. You'll love it!'

The Brother Superior folded his arms. 'You're avoiding the question. An *exact* figure.'

A long silence. And then: 'Two hundred. And fifty.'

The Brother in the green robe began to laugh, a wild, unnerving sound that made Charlie think of aliens throttling electric guitars.

The Brother Superior was shaking his head. 'You're the worst Brother in our history,' he growled. 'Get the rest of the things and take them to the altar. NOW!'

Inferior scuttled to do as he was bid.

Realising that the sacrificial altar must be the table he'd hidden under, Charlie tapped Wolfie on his metal nose and pointed back to their refuge. The robot dog's eyes flashed his understanding. Charlie crept back to the table and slipped underneath it again. Wolfie and Gruffles followed him.

CHAPTER TEN

C harlie sat still, trying to control his breathing, His fingers were clamped over Gruffles' muzzle and the dog was looking indignant.

Charlie heard a couple of muffled thuds directly above him, followed by a creak. *One of them's on the table!* He darted a warning glare at Wolfie, whose ear probes were straining upwards. Charlie shook his head. 'Keep still,' he mouthed.

And then the chanting began. Quietly to begin with, five voices intoned:

> *Brimstone, Grimstone, Bad and Bold,*
> *Evil weevil, Lust for Gold*
> *Devilish Dandy, Criminal Grandee*
> *All hail Sir Bryon!*

The voices rose towards the end of the chorus, echoing eerily off the rounded walls. Then the gruff voice of the Brother Superior rang out, alone, from on top of the table:

> *Bryon de Bohun, Lord of all crime*
> *Do not your followers fail*

Lead us to wealth and riches sublime
And keep us from landing in jail!

Once again, the five weird voices took up the chorus:
Brimstone, Grimstone, Bad and Bold,
Evil weevil, Lust for Gold
Devilish dandy, Criminal Grandee
All hail Sir Bryon!

Then it was back to the Brother Superior:
Dependables rot and Blaggardians crumble
Let us prevail, evil rules over all.
Let us succeed whilst Blaggardians grumble
Byron de Bohun, our Lord, hear our call!

There was one final chorus still to come, which was chanted with extra gusto:
Brimstone, Grimstone, Bad and Bold,
Evil weevil, Lust for Gold
Devilish dandy, Criminal Grandee
ALL HAIL SIR BRYON!

The chanting stopped. Beneath the table, Charlie could just imagine Milly rolling her eyes at him. *Evil weevil? Who made this stuff up?*

'We, the Brotherhood of Brimstone, worshippers of the Devilish Dandy, and followers of our wronged sister, Pecunia, pay you the ultimate tribute. We offer you – this chicken and ask that you look favourably on our plans to bring down Blaggard's!'

A long *EEEK* pierced the air. The noise was abruptly cut off. Something dark splatted onto the floor, just inside

Charlie's refuge. Gruffles made a lunge towards it. Charlie grabbed at his collar and held on to him. *Have we given ourselves away?*

Long seconds passed before he concluded that they were safe. He peered down at the stain, confused. It looked like blood. But rubber chickens didn't bleed!

Suddenly, the black blanket was pulled up. Charlie felt his heart stop for a second, then begin hammering wildly as he prepared for fight or flight. To one side of him, Wolfie was ready to spring into action. Gruffles seemed to be settling down for a nap.

A hand appeared briefly, clutching a mangled rubber chicken, coated in red. It flung the 'corpse' under the table and the blanket twitched back into place. Charlie let out a long, relieved breath and prayed that the sacrifice would bring the ceremony to an end.

There was a short silence and then the rumbling voice of the Brother Superior said: 'It's been a long day and my classroom is in a bit of a mess, so let's wind up the meeting now.'

Another teacher! Charlie thought.

'Inferior – make sure you get a big supply of tomato ketchup before our next ceremony. You can "feloniously acquire" it, as our departed Brother Nick liked to say, from the school kitchens, and fill all the chickens with it. It added a touch of realism.'

'Yes, Sir,' Inferior sounded relieved. 'I'll store the ketchup bottles under the altar. I know you like to keep the sacred cave tidy.'

Charlie froze. He saw five little indents jabbing into the

blanket, as fingers grabbed it. They began to lift it. He shot an imploring look at Wolfie. 'HELP!' he mouthed.

Wolfie's eyes gave a flash of yellow and he launched into action.

He nudged Gruffles, who leapt onto his back, bashing his head against the table and baring his fangs in a grimace of pain. His teeth glowed eerily. At the same time, Wolfie was disappearing. The last things to vanish were his eyes, which gave Charlie a brief red wink before fading into nothingness.

All this took about a second. As the blanket covering Charlie's hiding place was being lifted away, he had a brief glimpse of five pairs of feet and a wall of long robes.

Gruffles gave his most terrifying howl. The 'ghost dog' rocketed out. The terrified Brothers gave a collective shriek and ran. Charlie waited for a couple of seconds, savouring the racket made by five people careering around an enclosed space in a state of panic.

Then he peeked out.

The first thing he saw was Superior, peering behind him and running straight into one of the tall aerosols. It toppled to the ground, followed by the Brother. He must have fallen on the release button, because unhealthy-looking brown vapour hissed into the room. An overpowering sewage stench filled the room. Superior clamped a hand over his nose.

Interesting! Charlie thought, before the odour reached him. When it did, it drove all thoughts out of his head except *I'm gonna throw up*

Superior struggled back to his feet and hurtled for the

door, yelling *'BRIMSTONE!'* The other Brothers were just behind him.

The door swung open. The 'ghost dog' hung back just a little bit. All five of the Brotherhood shot outside and into the woods, which were now in total darkness.

Charlie climbed out, shielding his nose with his hands. He examined the toppled aerosol. 'PONG-O-RAMA– *INSTANT AIR STAGNATOR,'* he read out loud. 'Now that's *really* interesting.' He was careful to put it back as he'd found it. Then he gave each of the dogs – the living one and the robot one – a quick pat.

'Thanks guys. We'd better go and tell Milly.'

CHAPTER ELEVEN

After sneaking Gruffles back into his room and warning Wolfie to BEHAVE, Charlie went in search of Milly.

He found her in the Junior Common Room, the second noisiest place in the school, after the Library.

Today the room was especially busy. Music was blaring and a small crowd of spectators were watching Luke Yates, the self-proclaimed Genie of Gaming, working his magic. An old-fashioned arcade machine had been altered so that the robbers were the good guys, and the cops were the ones running over Dependables and shooting their way out of the most mundane situations, when really all they needed to do was walk away with a polite smiile.

William Proctor and Agatha Quint were among a noisy group who were just settling down to a game of No-Clue-D'Oh! You had to do everything in your power to stop the detective from solving the murder, whilst trying to gather together the implements to do away with him in the place and manner outlined on a randomly picked card.

Milly was standing slightly apart, staring at the relics of the extraordinary life of Sally Masters, eighteenth century Queen of the Highwaymen. One look at Milly's set profile told Charlie that she was not in a good mood.

Milly felt a special connection with Blunderbuss Sally, the highway name of Sally Masters, and Charlie often found her in this room, examining the mural showing scenes from Sally's life. There was Sally arm-wrestling with fellow highwaymen and leaping from the gallows onto the back of her galloping horse, White Wonder, aiming her blunderbuss at a dim-looking hangman. If the room was empty, Milly sometimes practised her lock picking skills on the cabinet that housed Sally's long, caped coat and tricorn hat. Sometimes she tried them on. Charlie had to admit that they suited her, although the coat dragged on the ground.

Jet Mannington, who as a Year Ten shouldn't have been there at all, was lounging on one of the sofas, trying to impress a yawning girl. At the same time he was keeping one wary eye on Flora Fairbrother, a deceptively wimpy looking Year Eight who, with some eager helpers, had recently come close to drowning him in soup, in a food fight. Flora was making loud references to *minestrone*.

To one side of the giant TV screen, a raucous pack of Year Eights were playing 'Pin the Pansy on Pecunia,' with a life-size cardboard cut out of Pecunia Badpenny. Blindfolded Blaggardians were guided up to it, waving a plastic flower. The challenge was to stick the flower onto the cut out. There was a howl of laughter as one boy removed his blindfold to find that the flower was stuck in one corner of Pecunia's mouth. She looked like a skinny goat chewing its lunch.

Suddenly Gabriel Huggins appeared in the doorway. His face was dark with anger as he glared at the cut out of Badpenny. '*What's* the meaning of this?' His voice was no longer timid – it was ringing with outrage.

Huggins hesitated for a moment, obviously struggling to regain his calm. His eyes darted round the room before coming to rest on Jet. 'Jet Mannington. You shouldn't be here. Get back to your own common room,' he said, in something like his usual tone.

Jet gave him a speculative glare and for a few seconds Charlie thought that he was going to disobey. But he got up and walked slowly past the teacher, and out into the corridor.

'Jolly good. Er ...' Huggins suddenly seemed to have run out of things to say. He gave a quick awkward smile and departed.

'You OK?' Charlie asked, coming to stand next to Milly.

'I'm fine. Angry. Huggins went out of his way to make me look stupid...' She clenched her fists. 'Just then – did you get the impression that it wasn't really Jet that he was angry at?'

Just for a second Charlie thought about the disguised teachers in the Sewage Room. Could there be a connection? Could Huggins be one of them? It didn't seem likely. He was the wrong size, for a start. And anyway, they worshipped Sir Bryon, not Badpenny. Charlie dismissed the thought.

'Chill, Mills,' he said. 'I admit – he did overdo the sarcasm with you, but – he's new. Give him a chance. And no. I didn't think that it wasn't Jet he was angry at. Jet makes everyone angry!'

Milly's eyes darkened. 'He's up to something. Cheating somehow. I don't know how, but I'm gonna find out. And he reminds me of someone. I can't think who yet, but I'll remember if it kills me.' She hesitated for a second. 'Change the subject, before we fall out again. Did you get Gruffles in?'

'I did, but I had a bit of an adventure on the way. Come on, we need to talk.' He guided her out of the room, exchanging a swift glance with Agatha Quint as he passed the No-Clue-D'oh! players.

'You're cheating!' William Proctor was protesting to Sophie the blackmailer. 'You can't kill him with the exploding soap, the faulty hairdryer *and* the icicle stuffed with poison. It's not fair. We want some weapons too...'

Milly and Charlie wandered round the school, passing the Library which was noisier than Borage Bagpuize Open Air Swimming Pool on a hot Saturday in July, and then through Reception, with its portraits of ugly Sir Thomas Blaggard and beautiful Sir Bryon de Bohun.

Now that Sir Bryon's Brain was so much in his thoughts, Charlie spotted a detail in the portrait that he'd never noticed before – the glint of a gold chain behind the Dandy's elaborate cravat. *I guess the Brain was suspended from that.*

They walked over the mosaic floor depicting scenes from the school's long history, and down another corridor leading past the Forgery and Betrayal classes towards the Assembly Hall. As they walked, Charlie outlined what he'd just witnessed.

'...I got out of there pretty quickly. But they're up to no good. For some reason, they want to complete Badpenny's plan to destroy Blaggard's,' Charlie finished.

Milly was frowning. 'I bet it was them who pinched the Brain. It would make sense. Did you say that they called Badpenny their sister?'

'Yes, but I don't think they mean it literally. They call each other Brothers, and I bet they're not related.'

'Maybe not. We'll look into it, anyway.'

Milly stopped walking and stared at the plaster death mask of Findlay Foggarty, the body snatcher. It was among a long line of similar masks, all taken from famous Blaggardians just after their luck had run out for the final time. Judging from the look of affront on his face, death had been little more than an annoyance to Foggarty.

'There are two things we need to concentrate on,' Milly said. 'The first one is Gruffles. The Brotherhood has obviously got it in for him. But we've got to send him into the woods – Blaggard's needs its ghost dog. Anyway, he can't stay in your room all day, for obvious reasons. So – remember those little mini cameras you were making for Espionage practice? Have you still got one that works?'

Charlie nodded. 'Loads.'

'Great. Link one to your laptop and fix it to Gruffles' collar. We'll be able to see everything that Gruffles does. Maybe he'll spot the Brotherhood again. Maybe they won't be so heavily disguised next time. And if he does get into trouble, we'll know.'

'Good idea. Pity they don't pick up sound too.' Charlie considered this for a few moments. 'Although the idea of listening to Gruffles' stomach gurgling all day is a bit off putting... So that's thing one. What's thing two?'

Milly turned away from the death mask and resumed wandering towards the Assembly Hall.

'We need to find out who the Brotherhood are. We might find out from Gruffles' camera, but we can't rely on it. So – we're going to investigate.

'Let's find out how many teachers were holding detentions tonight. If Molesworthy's the only one, it's easy. But I don't think we'll be that lucky. Detentions at Blaggard's are usually fuller than normal classes. When we meet a teacher, we'll bring the word *BRIMSTONE* into the conversation and see how they react.' There was a flush of colour on Milly's cheeks.

She's excited, Charlie realised. *She loves a challenge.* Aloud, he said, 'OK. Although how we'll bring Brimstone into every conversation, I don't know.'

'We'll think of something,' Milly replied. 'Let's start checking out the teachers. Hope you remember your interrogation techniques. Come on.' She headed for the Staff Room.

CHAPTER TWELVE

The Staff Room door was snatched open before Milly had finished knocking. Miss Vipond stood there, glaring. She was wearing a fluffy dressing gown in her favourite beige and she'd released her hair from its usual tight bun. It was sticking out from her head like an abandoned stork's nest. The aroma of hot cedar wood wafted from behind her.

Milly heard Charlie gulp. He had a hate-hate relationship with the Defiance and Discourtesy teacher, who was constantly trying to goad him into rudeness. Charlie avoided Miss Vipond as much as possible.

'Dillane and Partridge,' Miss Vipond had the unique ability to make *anything* sound like an insult. 'What? Make it fast – I was about to have a sauna and massage. I'm feeling a bit tense.' She made a little sideways movement with her neck. It clicked.

'We wanted to ask you something –,' Milly began.

Jane Vipond's brows drew together. 'I assumed you

hadn't disturbed me just to remind me about how useless you are.'

Milly wasn't going to be intimidated. *No point using subtlety with Miss Vipond. She wouldn't even notice.* She gave Miss Vipond a serene smile. 'We've been talking about something we heard in a lesson a few days ago,' she said. 'Something about a secret society started by Sir Bryon de Bohun. The Brotherhood of – ? We can't remember. Windblown? Shinbone?'

'Brimstone. The Brotherhood of Brimstone,' Charlie interjected, with his best innocent look. 'I've just remembered. We wanted to find out all about it –'

'You've made me lose my place in the queue for the sauna for *this*? I was nearly at the front, and Herman Blight was straight behind me. He'll be in there for ages, with his curling tongs!' Miss Vipond snapped. 'I've got no idea what you're talking about. Someone's making up Fabrications. Which teacher was it?

'Um, Mr Borgia, I think,' Milly looked puzzled. 'Yes, that's right. He was saying that his great grandmother was nearly sacrificed by this Brotherhood thingy. But his great granddad made a plane out of fish bones and got her out just in time. I *think* that was it, wasn't it, Charlie?'

'No. Not fish bones, you idiot. Chicken bones!' There was a gleam in Charlie's eyes. Milly relaxed a little. *It's OK. We're working together again. We've had our differences recently, but we're still a team.*

Miss Vipond shook her head in disbelief. 'Unbelievable. Whenever I think that you might be making some progress towards criminality, you say something so stupid it takes my breath away. You *believed* Mr Borgia? Even I don't believe a word he says and I'm his – close friend.'

She started closing the door. Then she stopped. 'And Partridge, "idiot" is an insult I teach to the Tiny Tyrants on their very first day. If that's the best you can do, you'll be joining them.' She slammed the door in their faces.

They turned and walked away in silence. When they were sure they were out of earshot, Charlie asked: 'What do you think?'

'Suspicious. Very. If she wasn't involved, she'd have flattened us for wasting her time.' Milly said. 'She's a potential Brother for sure. We're off to a great start!'

Their next target was Edgar Borgia. On their way to the Fabrication classroom, they came across Gabriel Huggins, sticking a poster to one of the doors that opened onto Reception.

COMING SOON:

DECEPTION CLUB

PREPARE TO BE DECEIVED, DUPED AND DELUDED!

'Sir, don't all those words mean the same thing?' Milly asked.

'Of course not,' Huggins answered. 'They're completely different, as anyone but an idiot would know.'

'Please can you explain the difference? In words of one syllable. I'm obviously an idiot,' Milly said.

Huggins got even pinker. He looked at his watch. 'I'm far too busy to waste my time. Go and find a dictionary.' He scurried away, avoiding Milly's eyes.

'He's the idiot,' Milly commented, curling her lip.

They found Mr Borgia redoing his soundproofing, which took frequent batterings from Blaggardians who tended to get overexcited when hooked up to his truth detectors. 'Oh yes, I'm a member of the Brotherhood,' he beamed. 'How did you find out? I can't quite remember the full name of the sect, but that's just because we're always too busy murdering and blackmailing and intimidating and...'

Milly raised her eyes to the ceiling. She and Charlie walked away, leaving Borgia to his Fabrications.

The next teacher they came across was Mr Molesworthy, shuffling along short-sightedly.

'Who's that?' he snuffled, as Milly and Charlie approached him. 'Oh Mr Dillane and Miss Partridge. Or is it the other way around? What can I do for you?'

Milly had decided to base their interrogation of Molesworthy around Forgery – the subject closest to his heart. 'As you know, we're Vice-Captains of Martinet House and we're trying to come up with a brilliant idea for Founders' Day,' she began.

'We're both fascinated by Forgery and by the school's amazing history,' Milly crossed her fingers that he hadn't spotted her asleep in her last Forgery lesson. 'So we're trying to combine both of those things in our idea. We're wondering if we can show some famous Blaggardians involved in Forgery. Something really exciting.' Milly could feel Charlie shaking, as he struggled to stop himself from bursting into giggles at the thought of an *exciting* Forgery presentation.

Molesworthy's face was wreathed in smiles. 'Excellent. It's so seldom my specialism is appreciated. What can I do to help?'

'Charlie mentioned that in one of his Advanced Hacking classes, he'd got into the top-secret files of a government criminologist called – Basil – what was the last name, Charlie?' Milly turned suddenly to Charlie, who was making little snorting noises behind her.

Charlie stopped snorting and gaped. 'Eh?' Milly gave him a straight-faced nod. 'Oh, right. Basil, er, Basil – Grufflington. I think that was it... Actually, it was a one of those double-barrelled names. Basil Grufflington-Dogsworthy,' he said, warming to the subject.

'What an unusual name,' Molesworthy commented. 'And what did you find in the files of Mr Grufflington-Dogsworthy?'

Milly took over again. 'What he found was a lot of hush-hush research about a secret society that used to be based here at Blaggard's. The Brotherhood of – what was it, Charlie?'

'Brimstone,' Charlie supplied. 'Anyway, one of the Brothers Brim, or whatever they called themselves, was a great forger. I couldn't find out his name.'

'So,' Milly continued, 'we were just wondering if you knew anything about this Brotherhood thingy, or the great Blaggardian forger? We'd like to get the details right for Founders' Day.'

The Forgery teacher blinked hard. 'The Brotherhood,

you say. It was Brotherhood, wasn't it? No. I don't know anything. Never heard of it. I don't think it would be a suitable subject. Not at all...' He scuttled away.

'We've got two definite suspects now,' Milly said, as she and Charlie headed towards their bedrooms. 'Basil *Grufflington-Dogsworthy*? Glad you stuck to gritty realism.'

Charlie gave an apologetic shrug. 'Sorry. You sprung it on me. I'd just been thinking about fitting the camera to Gruffles' collar and I'd decided to call it the Gruffles-Cam. My mind doesn't move as fast as yours. I can't leap from subject to subject like a cat burglar on a hot tin roof! '

Huggins was in Reception again as they passed through on their way to the stairs. He was examining the poster he'd put up a short time earlier.

'Any more thoughts on the wording, Sir?' Milly couldn't resist asking.

'The wording of this poster? What's wrong with it?' he asked. Without waiting for a response, he hurried away, leaving Milly and Charlie staring at each other.

'I'm starting to get an idea about what's happening,' Milly said. 'I just need a bit of time to work it out.'

CHAPTER THIRTEEN

The following morning was Gruffles' first day of haunting with the Gruffles-Cam attached to his collar. He was alone, because Wolfie had gone off to Greenland to rescue a small flock of sheep. They had wandered onto a punt, which had drifted into the middle of huge thermal lake, heated by a geyser. Wolfie had projected a news item about the unfortunate sheep onto the wall in Milly's room, when Charlie called for her before breakfast. According to the reporter, all attempts to rescue the sheep had failed, and it wouldn't be long before the steaming geyser turned them into boiled mutton. Already they were looking very hot and bothered. Wolfie had flown off in invisibility mode, after a perped promise to return before lights out.

After a quick breakfast, there was time to return to Charlie's room to check on Gruffles' progress. Charlie and Milly sat on his bed and watched as his laptop flickered into life.

The camera was transmitting clearly and they were

treated to a dog's eye view of the woods. It took a little while to get accustomed to the way the camera jiggled as Gruffles trotted around, occasionally stopping to examine a long-dead mole or crouching to stalk a pigeon. Once he stopped next to a large tree. After a few seconds, swirls of steam began to billow around the camera in the cold October morning.

'Nice,' Milly said. 'The perfect start to the day – watching the aftermath of your dog taking a pee.'

'It could be worse,' Charlie said, his voice heavy with meaning.

There was one moment of excitement, when the Gruffles-Cam captured two people moving through the trees. Gruffles followed them. Milly and Charlie held their breath, hoping for a glimpse of a monkish robe, perhaps even a flash of face beneath a hood.

What they got instead was the expanse of Edgar Borgia's domed forehead as he frolicked through the foliage, dressed in his usual hand-knitted jumper. Once he stopped and ducked behind a bush, then jumped out to surprise his companion.

The Gruffles-Cam captured the second figure's lower half first – it wore a long, garment that dragged over the newly fallen leaves. 'It *looks* like one of the Brotherhood.' Charlie said. Then Gruffles changed position and they saw the second figure's face. It was Miss Vipond, in her dowdy dress.

Milly and Charlie watched Jane Vipond's mouth open in a shriek as Borgia ambushed her. Her retaliation seemed automatic, sweeping Borgia's legs from under him with a vicious kick. He tumbled to the ground. Miss Vipond put her hands to her mouth and dropped beside him. Borgia's lower lip was sticking out. *He's sulking!* Miss Vipond helped him up and dusted leaves off the back of his jumper. Then the pair clasped hands and skipped off together.

There was a long silence. 'That,' Milly said, 'was the single most disturbing thing I've ever seen. Give me Gruffles peeing against a tree, any day of the week. Or Pecunia Badpenny promising murder and mayhem.'

Charlie nodded vehemently.

The morning was uneventful and at lunchtime, after counting the number of teachers who'd held detentions the previous evening, which ran into double figures, Milly and Charlie decided to change into Dependable clothing and take a walk into the sleepy town of Borage Bagpuize.

'I know we're not allowed to the leave the grounds without permission, but the change of scene will do us good,' Milly said. 'And anyway, Ms Martinet should be delighted that we're breaking the rules!'

Dressed in jeans and sweatshirts, they sneaked through a back door and made their way round to the path intersecting the woods. Passing the Science Labs they came across an elderly window cleaner, scrubbing enthusiastically at the sparkling glass. 'Hello, Mr Huggins,' Milly called, eliciting an annoyed glare from the man.

Charlie's jaw dropped. 'How did you know it was him? He looks totally different.'

'He can't disguise his nose. At least, not very well. Anyway, can you imagine Ms Martinet letting a *window cleaner* inside Blaggard's?'

At the end of the path, they punched in the security code that opened the infamous Twisted Gates, and set off for town.

The Dependable world seemed calm after the madness of Blaggard's: cars drove by at reasonable speeds; people smiled at each other without ulterior motives; others who were oddly dressed were just people with weird taste – not villains disguised for their next criminal exploit.

They passed Moira's Woole shoppe, and the store selling candles that smelt of everything except wax. Over the road was a shop that had been empty since Milly and Charlie had arrived in Borage Bagpuize. Now the cloudy windows had been cleaned and were crammed with junk. Old record players, creepy showroom dummies, piles of books, heavy old-fashioned phones, a stuffed pheasant wearing a tartan waistcoat, cardboard boxes full of – who knew what. Above the window, the shop's name was painted in plain black letters:

W.O.R.N.O.U.T

'Wornout? What kind of a name is that?' Charlie asked.

Milly shrugged. 'Dunno. Let's find out.' She led Charlie across the road, pulling up short while an old lady on a bike, transporting a dog in a wicker basket, laboured past.

A bell pinged as Milly pushed the door. A second later, a man appeared from a recess at the back of the shop.

'Hi, guys,' he said, in a depressed voice. 'You're welcome to look around. Although I don't think you'll find anything

to interest you.' As he came forward Milly saw th
quite young, with stooped shoulders and a defer

'Hi. Nice shop. Interesting name,' she said, pic..
a twisting, pencil-shaped piece of metal about the length
of her hand.

'It stands for Weird Old Rubbish No One Uses Today,'
the man replied. 'I always tell the exact truth. Not that
it gets me anywhere.' He glanced at the object Milly was
examining. 'That's for curling moustaches. You wouldn't
like it.' He looked over at Charlie, who had bent to stand
inside what looked like a plastic space helmet attached to
a long upright pole, mounted in a stand. 'That's an old hair
dryer from the 1960s. It makes your hair go really wild. You
don't need it,' he said.

'Er, thanks,' Charlie replied, ducking to remove himself
from the hairdryer. 'The last thing I need is wilder hair!'

'True. So, do you go to Borage Bagpuize High School?'
the depressed man asked, in a manner that suggested
that he couldn't care less, but he knew he should make
conversation.

'No. We go to Constance Bottomley's Academy for the
Rural Arts,' Milly said, darting warning looks at Charlie.
Mention of the school's true identity was forbidden in
Dependable company.

'Oh, the hippy place on the road out of town? It sounds
like a waste of everyone's time to me... What are your
favourite lessons?'

Milly thought furiously. 'I like creative haystack building.
Charlie here's a whizz at sheep topiary.'

The man nodded. 'Completely pointless, but I can see

73

the attraction. Looks like Charlie should aim some of those topiary skills at his own head!' Then he sighed. 'I don't mean to be rude. I just can't help it.'

Milly felt a bit sorry for the depressed man with his hopeless conversation. 'No offence taken, is there Charlie?' Charlie shook his head, lips twitching. 'Never go in for a career in advertising, though, will you?' she continued.

The man looked embarrassed. 'Actually, guys, I was in advertising until recently. It didn't work out.' He stared at the floor for a moment. 'I was responsible for the Wipe-Ease ads,' he confessed.

'Ew,' Milly and Charlie said together. The previous year's TV ads for Wipe-Ease toilet paper had traumatised the nation. Even though the ads had used cartoon squirrels rather than humans to demonstrate Wipe-Ease's Ultra Absorbant Efficiency, the images had been all too graphic. Help-lines and charities had been set up for those worst affected by the brutally factual adverts. Even now, mention of the brand name made people flinch and clench their bum cheeks.

Seeing the man's shoulders droop even more, Milly said, 'Never mind. You created something unforgettable. You should be proud.'

Charlie gave a snort of laugher, which he tried unsuccessfully to turn into a cough. To cover his embarrassment, he knelt down and started rummaging through a box of dusty objects.

Relieved to have an excuse to get away from the drippy man, Milly bent over to join him. She turned over old pot lids, strings of broken beads, china figurines with missing extremities.

And then her fingers fastened on something heavy and cube-shaped that just fitted into her palm. It felt smooth like glass but it was warm. She pulled it out and blew some of the dust off. There was flowing writing engraved on each of its surfaces. *Dunno what it is but I like it. Wonder if there's any more?* She rummaged again and found another one, a little chipped around the edges. And then one more, more battered still. *I'll buy them. Maybe it will cheer the poor man up a bit.*

She took them over to the man and held out her hand. 'How much for these?' she said.

He gave them a brief glance and shrugged. 'They're worthless. 50p? I bought them recently from a pair of weird twins who were moving to the area. They were getting rid of a lot of rubbish at a car boot sale. They're in terrible condition, like the rest of the tat I bought from them. '

Milly felt in her jeans for some money. She dropped a coin into his palm. 'Thanks,' she said, putting the dusty objects into her bag and turning to leave. 'We'd better get back to school, Charlie. Don't want to be late for nettle-weaving class!'

Charlie stood up and wiped the dust from his hands. 'My second favourite lesson! See you again. Good luck with the shop!' he called.

'I expect it will fail miserably. I won't be planning any exotic holidays...'

CHAPTER FOURTEEN

That evening, Milly and Charlie were combing the woods, looking for Gruffles. They were a little later than usual – the afternoon had been busy, finishing with a meeting with Jet Mannington to discuss their contribution to the Founders' Day celebrations.

It hadn't gone well. Jet wasn't the brightest spark, but he believed that he was. 'He's like Gruffles when he gets hold of one of my socks,' Charlie said afterwards. 'You can drag him round by it. You can lift him up by it. He won't let go, no matter what.'

Jet's idea for Founders' Day was astonishing in its simplicity. 'A mud-wrestling match. Between Sir Thomas Blaggard and Sir Bryon de Bohun,' he announced, with obvious pride.

Silence.

Eventually Milly said: '...That's interesting. Different. But, do you think Ms Martinet would like it?'

'Uh, yes?' Jet gave her a look of pity. 'Isn't it obvious? She'd *love* to see me wrestling.'

Things began to make sense. Jet was the star of the school mud-wrestling club. He was always beating up Eric Ponsonby, the wrestling instructor, who'd been heard in the lunch queue trying to persuade Jane Vipond to take over the duty from him.

'Right. So – who would you be – Blaggard or de Bohun? Have you decided?' Charlie asked. He had an odd, pursed look around his lips. *He's trying not to laugh*, Milly realised, struggling to swallow her own giggles.

'Yes, of course I have. Do I *look* stupid? I'd be Sir Thomas Blaggard. He was the top villain of his day. Just like I'm gonna be. He was nasty and strong, like me.'

Milly clutched his sleeve. 'But, have you thought this through? Sir Thomas was ugly. Really ugly.'

Jet's face fell. 'I hadn't thought about that... I'll have to be Sir Bryon!'

Milly pretended to think for a few moments. 'OK, he wasn't ugly. And he was evil. But – he was a bit of a wimp. Would you feel comfortable, playing a wimp?'

'A wimp! I'm not playing a wimp. Why did you even waste my time suggesting it, Dillane?'

'Sorry – stupid me!' She waited for a moment and then said: 'Maybe we – er – *you* should come up with a different plan?'

Jet's forehead furrowed with concentration.

After a few minutes, his brow cleared. 'Got it! Sir Thomas and Sir Bryon versus Godzilla. In a mud-wrestling match. I'll be Godzilla. It'll be epic!'

Milly suppressed a sigh. She looked at her watch. 'We'll

meet again soon and talk about it some more. We've – got to go and see a man about a dog.'

Jet's stupidity was forgotten as they searched the woods for Gruffles.

'It's just not like him not to come when he hears me,' Charlie fretted. 'Actually, that's not entirely true. Sometimes he'll come straight up. Other times he'll think it's a chasing game and dash off through the trees. What he never does is nothing. It's just not in his nature!'

Milly thought for a few moments. 'Have you got any LEAP in your pocket? Maybe if you rattle it around a bit...?'

LEAP was Gruffles' favourite food. Recently, Charlie had discovered a liking for it, too, after he'd been forced to eat some during a room inspection. It was either that or give away the fact that he was hiding a dog. Milly knew that he usually carried a few nuggets of it around, in case he got the munchies.

Charlie dug around in his pockets. He pulled out one lump of LEAP. 'Great. How do we rattle one piece of dog food?'

'Bash it against a stone?' Milly suggested.

'I don't think you're taking this seriously,' he said, looking offended.

'Sorry. Tell you what – let's go back to your room and check out the Gruffles-Cam. If that fails, Wolfie'll be back soon. He'll track Gruffles down faster than Miss Vipond can think up an insult!'

In five minutes, they were in Charlie's room. Charlie went straight to his laptop to access the Gruffles-Cam.

The scene that flickered to life wasn't what either of

them had been expecting. Instead of trees they saw brick walls, brightly lit but with deep shadows in the corners. Gruffles shuffled a little, as if movement was difficult. The edge of a table came into view. It was draped with some kind of dark cloth. Beyond the table, standing against one curving wall, was a safe and some big cardboard boxes with the words 'TADDY'S – THE KETCHUP OF KINGS' printed on them. Next to these were half a dozen large aerosols, and a misshapen dummy in a glass case.

Charlie was on his feet. 'That's where the Brotherhood meet up!'

They could only watch as two figures came into view. One – the Brother Superior in his embroidered robe – moved forwards. He stopped in front of the Gruffles-Cam. The ends of a rope flicked in and out of Milly and Charlie's view. The camera shook as if Gruffles was barking. 'He's tied up!' Charlie exclaimed. The figure pulled back one hand and then brought it down with force. It would have hit Gruffles somewhere behind his head. The camera flinched.

Charlie was rushing to the door.

Milly put a restraining hand on his arm, but he shook her off. 'Get off me! They're torturing him! I've got to help him!'

CHAPTER FIFTEEN

Wolfie had had a fun day rescuing the overheated sheep, and now he was on his way home. The animals had been determined to show their gratitude by nibbling at his ears and it had taken a while to shake them off. In the end he'd had to *PERP* loudly to get them to leave him alone. They had trotted away with backward looks of reproach, but even so he suspected that he was now some kind of sheep god in Greenland. He did a jaunty loop the loop as he considered how much life had improved recently.

He flew at a leisurely pace, skimming across an icy lake and through a waterfall, to wash off the sheep saliva. For most of the time he stayed in invisibility mode for the sake of convenience, although he did materialise briefly to spook a pair of seagulls who were squabbling in the air over a half a herring.

For a creature as powerful as Wolfie, the journey wasn't especially taxing. But it was boring, and Wolfie hated being bored. He passed the time reflecting on his amazing luck in finding friends as good as Milly and Charlie. And Gruffles. Wolfie adored Gruffles.

Gruffles had shown him that a dog's life didn't have to mean being pushed around and bullied into terrifying humans, who, with a few exceptions, Wolfie rather liked. Gruffles had taught Wolfie to have fun, to disobey people when he felt like it and, above all, to value friendship and loyalty. Gruffles would die for Charlie – it was obvious. Wolfie knew that *he* would die for Gruffles, although he'd rather not, if there was an alternative.

When the waves of distress hit him, engulfing his ice-rimed body and nearly knocking him out the sky, he plummeted a thousand feet before he managed to master himself. In that time he'd processed the signals. He knew who was making them, where they were coming from and what he needed to do.

Gruffles was being attacked – was in pain. He was in the room that was used by the strange humans who liked to wear long dresses – the ones who played with rubber birds and sprayed smells that other humans didn't like. They were hurting his friend on purpose!

Wolfie gathered all his energy and prepared to use ultra-hypersonic speed. This was an emergency measure and there was a price to pay for using it. His energy sources would be completely depleted by the time he got to Borage Bagpuize. But Wolfie wasn't a worrier. The important thing was that he'd get back much faster to rescue his friend.

With a *PERP* so massive that it parted the waves and made the rocks on the ocean floor tremble, he blurred into the atmosphere.

Gruffles was frightened.

He'd been in this place before and that time it had been fun, chasing the humans around with Wolfie. He'd targeted this particular group of humans many times in the past weeks, and they always played along nicely – shrieking and running away as if they actually found him scary.

But this time they had the upper hand and it seemed that they hadn't really liked playing the chasing game at all, because they were punishing him for it. Hurting him. The blow on a tender area of his back was so painful that he'd let out a tremendous howl of agony and confusion. That seemed to be the right thing to do, because the human in the dress had turned away, muttering something about *That should do the trick.*

Gruffles tried to lick his sore place, but his bonds prevented him from reaching them. He shifted his body as much as he could and looked around the room. He was hungry and his tummy rumbled. The human who'd hit him had gone around the corner with the other one – the little one who smelled of fear.

He managed to look upwards at the thing that was suspended over him. It swung slowly backwards and forwards. If the heavy thing dropped, it would fall on him. Hurt him again. Did the humans realise that? Surely not. Humans were kind to him. Usually.

He tried to wriggle away, but he couldn't move his legs. All he could do was wait. Soon Charlie would come. Charlie would untie him and stroke him and take him away. Then he would feed him. He would be safe again. Safe with Charlie and Wolfie.

Charlie would come soon.

Wouldn't he?

CHAPTER SIXTEEN

Milly and Charlie were rushing through the woods, towards the Sewage Container. The smell was atrocious and they were torn between breathing shallowly, which minimised the stench, or taking deep breaths to help keep up their speed.

'It'll disappear once we get inside,' Charlie promised, when Milly had sputtered over a mouthful of foul air.

They were sweating by the time they'd reached the container, despite the cold evening weather. Charlie marched straight up to it, but Milly grabbed his arm. 'Hold on for a sec. We need a plan. What if the room's full of Brothers? You're not going to do Gruffles any good if we're trussed up next to him.'

Charlie glared at her, clutching at his knees as he fought for breath. 'I don't care. I'll think of something. I'll...' he stopped and kicked at a tree in frustration. 'I don't know what I'll do. *Help me*, Mills.'

She stared into the distance for a few seconds. 'OK. How about this? Which of us is the fastest runner? I think it's you – you've had loads of practice chasing after Gruffles. And you know the woods better. And your legs are longer.'

'Agreed. Why?'

'What you should do is this – knock on the door. When someone opens it, say something that will make them really angry. They'll run after you, so you'd better be fast. While they're chasing you, I'll sneak inside and get Gruffles. You give them the slip. I'll meet you back in your room. OK?'

'It's not your best plan,' Charlie said, after a few moments of consideration. 'What if there are more of them than we saw on the Gruffles-Cam? What if they're all in there, and only some of them chase me?'

Milly gave a shrug. 'It's a chance we'll have to take. I'll improvise. Have you thought of something to say, to annoy them?'

'Yep. I'm ready.' He gave an uncertain smile.

'Have you got your mask with you? Good. Put it on. And smooth your hair down. You don't want to give them any clues about your identity... Good luck!'

Milly ducked behind a nearby tree and watched Charlie as he tied on his black mask and flattened his hair. He knocked on the door. There was a long silence. He knocked again, more urgently. She heard footsteps. The door opened. A figure appeared, its face hidden by its cowl.

'Hi,' Charlie said. 'I'm looking for a bunch of stupid grown-ups who like dressing up like nuns. Have you seen anyone like that? They've got a pathetic name – the Sisterhood of Soapstone, something like that. Someone told me that the reason this place smells so bad is that this Sisterhood never wash their pants. I've come to ask them if it's true.'

The cowled figure shook its head as if it thought it was hallucinating. 'WHAT? *Who* are you?' the alien voice said.

'I don't think I'm going to tell you that. You can call me Sir,' Charlie was starting to angle his body away from the Brother. *He's getting ready to run.* Milly edged closer.

Another cowled figure appeared in the gap in the door, behind the first one. 'What's going on?' This one had a gravelly voice.

'Oh hi,' Charlie said, lifting one hand. 'I guess *you're* the Sisterhood of Soapstone, judging by your pretty dresses. I just wanted to tell you that I've been customising the body of Sir Bryon de Bohun in the Assembly Hall. He looks *so* much better with pink bunny ears. And the wedding dress really suits him–'

With a roar of anger, the first Brother wrenched open the door and launched himself through it, closely followed by the Brother Superior. Charlie took to his heels.

Milly waited a second to check whether any more Brothers were going to appear. None did.

She crossed her fingers and slipped inside.

Gruffles was tied into a bundle on the floor, in front of the black-draped table. Directly above him was an old-fashioned metal safe, the size of a washing machine. It was suspended from the ceiling by a rope, which was threaded through a loop of rusting iron, set into the ceiling. It swung a little in a dangerous orbit, a few feet above Gruffles' body. Milly wondered what could be inside it, but there was a more pressing concern. The rope was creaking, as if the strain of holding up the safe was becoming too much for it.

Gruffles spotted Milly and gave a whimper of hope. She put her finger to her lips. Her eyes darted around the room. No one in sight. She crept over to the dog and caressed him behind his ears. 'Hi Stinky,' she whispered. 'What have they done to you?'

Gruffles gave a little whine.

She set to work on the ropes, which were tied in a tight knot in the middle of Gruffles' back. He flinched as she worked at them, and Milly spotted blood cloying around it. 'They've hurt you. They'll be sorry,' she promised in a whisper.

The knot was intricate. She managed to wiggle one of her long artist's fingers inside the central loop. It *was* loosening, but it was taking time. 'Come *on*,' Milly muttered to herself.

And then the door started to swing open. She muttered an oath. 'I'm not going far. I'll get you out of this,' she whispered to Gruffles. Giving the dog a final pat for courage, she slipped beneath the table.

CHAPTER SEVENTEEN

'Who was that boy?' a gravelly voice asked. 'I can't believe he gave us the slip. He looked tall – a Year Nine or Ten, maybe? We'll have to find him. And when we do, we'll get rid of him. He's insulted the Brotherhood. And he knows too much. A nice human sacrifice – just like the good old days!'

'Yes, Master,' an alien voice replied. 'We won't be needing any ketchup for that one!'

One of the pair clapped their hands with glee. 'Make it a priority... We can check on Sir Bryon in Assembly, in the morning. I'm almost sure that the boy was lying about the bunny ears...

Milly decided to risk a peep at the speakers. She edged the blanket to one side. They were standing more or less in front of her.

'This little incident aside, I think that things are going well,' the Brother who was speaking wore an embroidered black robe. 'We've got Sir Bryon's Brain, so we can destroy Blaggard's and kill Griselda Martinet whenever we want to.

We'll just keep her in suspense a little bit longer. It's fun, watching her get more and more haggard!' As he contemplated Ms Martinet's torture, one of his hands caressed his chin.

Hang on! Milly thought. *I think I've seen that gesture before!*

'I'm thinking we'll do it the day after Founders' Day. I believe that there'll be another humiliation coming her way that day, and I don't want to miss it. The more misery she experiences before she dies, the better.' The Brother in the embroidered robe gave a gravelly snigger. The other Brother was quick to join in.

'As well as that, we've proved that the ghost dog is just this stinking mongrel–' he kicked at Gruffles, making him yelp, '–with some help from the Wolf, who should be here pretty soon to rescue his friend. Then we'll capture him and tinker around with him a bit. When we've changed him into the Mole we'll be invincible! And now a human sacrifice, too. Christmas has come early!'

The Mole? Milly wondered how something could sound silly and threatening at the same time.

He'd hardly finished speaking before there was a *CRASH* that reverberated off the curved walls for ear-ringing seconds.

The door had been blown off its hinges and lay, buckled, on the floor. It landed inches from Gruffles, who was whimpering.

Neither of the Brothers was looking towards the table. They had been knocked off their feet and were lying on the floor, metres apart. Both appeared unhurt. Superior's cowl remained draped over his face, but Inferior's had slipped off his head.

Oho! Milly thought.

Wolfie flew into the room. But it wasn't Wolfie as Milly knew him – brimming with mischief and energy. He looked as if he'd expended every last jot of his power. His eyes were lightless black and he seemed to be having problems keeping to a straight line. His ears and tail probes trailed downwards. He landed next to Gruffles with a heavy thud. Gruffles gave a joyous bark and nosed his friend's cold body.

The Brother Superior jumped up and in a flash was at the wall, where the rope holding up the safe was tied off. From somewhere in his robe, he pulled out a long, curved knife.

'Hello Wolf. We were hoping you'd come. As you can see, your smelly friend is in a bit of a jam. This rope is very old and frayed and I don't know how long it will last, even if I don't...' He mimed sawing through the rope with the knife. 'We'll let the dog go, but only if you shut yourself down immediately. And I don't mean just pretend to shut down. I know the difference. Pecunia Badpenny left some very detailed blueprints.'

Even the mention of Badpenny could arouse no more than a brief flash of red in Wolfie's eyes. He gave a tiny, exhausted perp.

'I assume that's you agreeing. That's wise. This rope is on its last strands.' He sniggered, as if he'd said something hilarious. Inferior gave an obsequious giggle. Superior moved away from the rope and passed the knife over to

Inferior. 'There, your friend is safe,' he rumbled. 'I swear on the honour of the Brotherhood of Brimstone.'

Wolfie seemed to be assessing him. He gave a feeble wag of one of his tail probes for the benefit of his friend. And then all the light and life left him. One moment he was a living, thinking creature, albeit an exhausted one. The next, he was a just a chunk of cold metal, no more than an old piece of machinery to be abandoned in a junk yard. Gruffles gave a sorrowful whine.

Watching from under the table, Milly was biting her lip. She curled her fists, struggling not to throw herself onto the nearest Brother. *It won't help. There's two of them. They'll capture me and kill Gruffles anyway. We can find a way of rescuing Wolfie after I get Gruffles back to Charlie.*

'Lovely. He's ready to be pulled apart and made into something even more lethal,' Superior said, with satisfaction dripping from his voice. 'I'm going to go now, to work on my evil plans. I can't decide where to unleash the Mole first – The Houses of Parliament? The White House? The Kremlin? You clear up, Inferior. And make sure you kill the dog before you leave. The sacrificial knife is nice and sharp.'

'But – Master – what about all that "honour of the Brotherhood of Brimstone" stuff?' Inferior asked.

'You're a constant disappointment,' Superior was shaking his head. '*What* honour?'

He called out 'Brimstone' and strolled outside.

Milly swore under her breath. She would have to attack Inferior. She looked for something that she could use as a weapon.

The only thing under the table was a pitiful rubber

91

chicken. It looked as if it had been run over by a lawnmower and then dropped into a vat of something sticky. She picked it up and gave it a quick examination. *It'll have to do.*

Inferior had been testing the knife's sharpness on the fingers of his other hand. Now he was trying to turn Gruffles over, to expose his vulnerable tummy. Gruffles was snarling and resisting. He couldn't get away, but he whipped his head round and nipped Inferior's knife hand. Inferior swore and examined his wound.

Milly made her move. She launched herself from under the table, chicken swinging, and swiped Inferior round the head. Ketchup splurged out of the chicken's wounds. Inferior's glasses flew off. The knife soared against the wall, dropped to the floor and lay there, glittering in the artificial light.

Inferior let go of Gruffles and lifted his hands to feel his face. 'Blood!' he snarled. He whipped round to attack, but Milly was ready with the chicken. It whizzed through the air, catching him below his right ear. 'Ouch!' He dropped to his knees, groping around for his glasses. Milly got there first and brought one foot down on them, hard.

She scooped up Gruffles, bonds and all, and carried him towards the door. She stumbled a little under his weight. A second later, the frayed rope gave way and the safe crashed to the floor. Gruffles gave a yelp of fright.

'Brimstone!' Milly yelled. The door swung open. 'Wolfie, we're coming back for you!' she called out.

Holding Gruffles tight against her heart, she ran out into the night.

CHAPTER EIGHTEEN

C harlie hugged Gruffles for a long time when Milly got him back to his room. Then he set about releasing him from his bonds and cleaning his wound, which proved to be little more than a nasty cut. 'Although from the way he's whimpering and looking pathetic, you'd think he'd lost a leg, at least,' Milly remarked, lifting one eyebrow.

Charlie looked lovingly at his dog. 'He's always been a bit of a drama queen.' He gave Gruffles a pat. 'It looks like we've solved some problems and got some new ones.'

Milly nodded. 'Yep. We've got Gruffles back, and we know that it's the Brotherhood who stole the Brain, and that they want to destroy Blaggard's and Ms Martinet straight after Founders' Day. But we don't know *why*. And Wolfie's in big trouble. We need to rescue him. Fast. And find out who the other Brothers are.'

Charlie was scratching Gruffles' head. 'What's to stop us just sneaking back there tomorrow, during lessons? The teachers will be teaching. We could just pick Wolfie up and rescue him.'

'That's great if they're stupid enough to leave Wolfie unguarded. But I don't think they are,' Milly frowned. 'They all have breaks during the day – I bet they'll get a rota going. We know the identity of one of the Brothers now – Molesworthy. He has two free periods tomorrow – I've checked. The others will have free time too. Bet they can cover the whole day, between them.'

'They might hold ridiculous ceremonies, but I don't think they're stupid. So what do we do next? Rescue Wolfie? Find out who the other Brothers are? Report to Ms Martinet?' Charlie was pacing round his room.

'No!' Milly exclaimed. 'We don't tell anyone anything. I know we promised to report to Ms Martinet, but this is personal now and we'll sort it out ourselves. Huggins is involved in this, I can feel it. I think I've worked out how he does his lightning changes. I think there's two of them – twins!'

Charlie's mouth gaped. 'Twins! What a pair of cheats.'

'As for the rest of the plan, I need you to use your hacking skills and do two things. Look into Badpenny's family tree. There's got to be some reason the Brotherhood's so keen to finish off Blaggard's for Badpenny. I thought – hoped! – that she was an only child, but now I'm wondering if there might be a family connection between her and the Brotherhood... And then I want you to plant some information, rather than extract it. And it needs to be done quickly. For Wolfie's sake.'

Charlie ran a hand through his mop of hair and gave an ironic smile. 'No pressure, then! Just a normal day at Blaggard's!'

Milly grinned back. 'If we had a normal day, we'd be bored! And there's something else. They're hunting for you now – a tall boy, who they want to sacrifice. And maybe me, too. So, we need to be extra careful.'

Milly watched the smile disappear from Charlie's face. 'I'd forgotten that,' he said. 'I don't fancy being skewered as an offering to Sir Bryon.'

'If any teachers question you, be sure to act extra ignorant.'

'Shouldn't be hard,' Charlie said. 'I haven't got a clue what's going on in most of my lessons. But they're going to suspect us anyway. We've been asking about the Brotherhood.'

'Hmm. Yes, that was a mistake,' mentally, Milly kicked herself. 'Still, they won't want to sacrifice the wrong boy. It'll make new problems for them. So they'll double-check before doing anything. We'll just have to hope that we can sort this all out before they realise it was us!'

-oOo-

On the way to Assembly the following morning, Milly and Charlie bumped into Molesworthy. He emerged from an adjoining corridor, saw them coming and waited. Milly felt Charlie slow down.

'Keep going. And remember – we're ignorant,' she murmured.

'Hi, Sir,' Milly met Molesworthy with a wide smile. She let it fade. 'Wow! What's happened to your face?' A big bruise was blooming on Molesworthy's right cheek. He was wearing unusual glasses, too – glittery purple ones.

'Mr Partridge. Miss Dillane I was attacked. Last night.' He peered at them suspiciously. 'Where were you two yesterday evening?'

'Us? You can't suspect us? We were with William Proctor,' Milly Fabricated. 'He was helping us get to grips with the basics of Defiance and Discourtesy. Miss Vipond's fed up with us being so rubbish at it. Ask William – he'll back us up.'

Molesworthy gave a humourless smile. 'Believe me, I will. Tell me – what are your thoughts on dogs?'

Milly gave a shudder. 'Can't stand them,' she said. 'I've had a bit of phobia, ever since I was a little girl and my granny made me hide in a kennel with a drooling basset hound, during a police raid. It ruined my summer holiday. And my best dungarees!' She wrinkled her nose.

'And you, Mr Partridge?'

Charlie summoned a look of dim enthusiasm. 'Dogs? I love 'em... Actually that's not true. I don't like dogs much. But I love dog *food*. Eat it all the time. Mrs Christie will tell you!' Mrs Christie was the Boarding Mistress who'd found dog food in Charlie's room during an inspection.

'That reminds me...' he rummaged in his pocket and pulled out a handful of knobbly nuggets. 'I stocked up this morning – fancy a bit?' He blew away a bit of pocket fluff before offering the pile to Molesworthy.

'No! Thank you,' Molesworthy spluttered. He started to move on, but Milly stopped him with a question of her own.

'Er, Sir, those glasses. They're – unusual. Are they new?'

Molesworthy scowled. 'My own glasses were broken in

the attack. I had to go through Mr Huggins' disguise stocks for a pair with a similar prescription. These were the only ones strong enough. If anyone laughs... ' He stomped away.

When he'd gone a safe distance, Charlie said, 'That was a massive risk, Mills. What if Molesworthy checks with William Proctor?'

'Relax. It'll be fine. William will be so chuffed that he's someone's alibi, he'll definitely back it up. It makes him look really clever. He'll love that. Come on, let's see what Ms Martinet has to say.'

The Head Teacher was looking fiercer than ever, in a black trouser suit with glinting tiger's eye buttons that seemed a little baggier than it had been just a week ago. Her eyes, although underscored with heavy black smudges, still flashed with fierce intelligence.

She strode to the centre of the stage and started without preamble: 'If there is one rule at Blaggard's – one golden rule – it's the one about Honour Among Thieves. You all know this. YES?' she glared around.

All round the hall, Blaggardians nodded.

'Marvellous. So, I'm *ab-so-lutely* disgusted to report a theft on school premises. Someone has broken into the kitchens and stolen a year's supply of ketchup!' She scowled again.

'Not only does this show complete disrespect for our sacred rule, it's also completely pointless! If you're going to break a rule, break it for something worth having – Mr Nightingale's Crimtech gold watch with built-in poison darts, or a lethal weapon from the Sixth Form block – not for a pile of sauce bottles!' She shook her head in disbelief.

'When I find the culprit, they'll be expelled immediately and sent to Crumley's! I'll be checking everyone for red stains around their mouths.'

She let the threat sink in for a long moment. 'The only other thing I have to say is that Founders' Day is nearly here and I'm still waiting for one house to submit their ideas for spectacular parental entertainment. Blaggard and De Bohun Houses – your plans have been considered and passed, with a few reservations.' She paused for a second, seeming to consider them.

'Martinet House – Jet Mannington, Milly Dillane and Charlie Partridge – get your skates on. And no, Mr Mannington, mud-wrestling is NOT acceptable, no matter what kind of fancy dress you're wearing!'

Milly saw Jet glaring at her. 'Looks like Jet's going to blame us for his stupid wrestling plan,' she said to Charlie. 'He must've told Ms Martinet about it when we were busy.'

'Great,' Charlie groaned. 'Nothing's ever Jet's fault. Still, at least we won't have to make fools of ourselves by rolling around in a muddy sandpit.'

'–Don't let me down. I'm not in the mood for it.' Ms Martinet finished. She turned and headed for the steps, but at the last moment she stopped and looked back.

'One more thing. Certain students – they know who they are – have offered assistance in a private matter of mine. I hope they're making progress, because time is running out. For everyone.'

CHAPTER NINETEEN

Milly was in a Betrayal lesson, without Charlie. He'd had all of his Betrayal and some of his Plotting lessons cut, partly to give him extra time for his specialities, Hacking and Advanced Criminal Electronics and Engineering, subjects in which he was already the best pupil in the school, and partly because he was considered so hopeless in certain subjects that he might as well spend his time doing something more useful.

Marius Babington, the Betrayal teacher, always reminded Milly of the portrait of Guy Fawkes that was hanging in the 'Inspirational Lives' section of the Library, and she suspected that he cultivated the similarity on purpose. There did seem to be quite a few posters of Fawkes in the Betrayal classroom, along with others with helpful tips on facial expressions and inspirational quotes such as:

'It is easier to forgive an enemy than to forgive a friend'

**SO DON'T MAKE ANY FRIENDS AND YOU'LL
ALWAYS BE FORGIVEN!**

Milly quite looked forward to Betrayal lessons, and tried hard to hide the fact that she had no more intention of betraying anyone than Babington had of becoming decent, reliable sort of person.

William Proctor came to sit next to Milly, as he often did now that Charlie was no longer there. As soon as Babington's back was turned, she'd asked him about providing an alibi for the previous night. 'Mr Molesworthy's got an idea that we're mixed up in the Great Ketchup Robbery,' she said, with a mysterious smile.

A flush of gratification settled on Proctor's freckly cheeks. 'Of course. Only too delighted,' he said. 'In fact, why don't you pop up to my room later and I'll give you some genuine Discourtesy tuition? To add veracity to your alibi? Bring a bottle of ketchup or two with you. You never know when it'll be useful.'

Milly had made a vague excuse and decided that the next time she went into Borage Bagpuize, she'd buy William a bottle of ketchup. *I'll have to make sure it's the same brand – Taddy's, was it? – or he'll know it wasn't stolen! I'd hate to shatter his illusions.*

The lesson began with Babington drawing a large, upwards-pointing triangle on the whiteboard. Then he added horizontal lines to divide it into five sections.

'I call this the Scale of Betrayal,' he said, stroking his pointy beard. 'What I want you to do is this – think of all the types of people you might be called on to betray during your career as a master criminal. If you come up with more than five, that's fine. Just add more lines to your triangle. Then rank them in order of ease of betrayal. The better you know someone, or the more highly you regard them, the further up the scale they go. When you've decided on your order, write them inside the sections in the triangle.' He demonstrated on the whiteboard.

'People it would be easy to betray – strangers, people you hate, etc, go in the bottom, where the triangle is widest. Those you would really have to force yourself to betray – family? friends? – go right at the top. You'll keep these pages in your folders, and every time you reach a new level on your personal Betrayal Scales, you get a reward – a voucher for money off at Cloak and Dagger – boutique for the Felonious Famous. Off you go...'

Milly chewed her pen. Next to her, William Proctor was filling both sides of a sheet of paper with the names of people he was prepared to betray. Her mind wandered. She hoped that that Wolfie would be OK until they launched their rescue plan. *We should be ready tomorrow. Just need to make sure that they've picked up the fake info. And to break into the Disguise classroom. And the science labs, too.*

She started thinking about what she'd overheard while she was rescuing Gruffles. The Brotherhood wanted to turn Wolfie into a Mole. A lethal Mole. What on earth for? What would such a thing even look like?

Hardly aware of what she was doing, her pen began flying. Soon there was a nightmare creature on her paper – streamlined, with huge, lethally sharp hands for digging and a pointed corkscrew nose that could drill through anything and anyone in its way.

William Proctor nudged her. 'Doodling again, Milly? Anyone would think that you wanted to be an artist, not a leading exponent of the felonious arts.' He laughed at his own joke.

Milly looked down at the monster she'd been drawing. She thought of friendly, mischievous Wolfie, who loved to levitate Gruffles and save Dependables and who sometimes looped the loop with sheer joy. *If it's the last thing I do, I'm going to rescue Wolfie. He saved us from Badpenny. I owe him.*

She looked up and caught Babington's eye. He lifted his arched eyebrows enquiringly. She gave him a quick apologetic smile, screwed up her drawing and lobbed it into a nearby bin. Then she quickly jotted down some meaningless names. Babington quirked his lips and gave her a tiny wink. He continued the lesson.

-oOo-

Meanwhile, Charlie was in Advanced Criminal Electronics and Engineering – or ACEE for short, with his favourite teacher, Herman Blight, aka the Wild Haired Wizard. Blight had earned his nickname because of his hair, which was carefully arranged to appear ungovernable, and because he was a total genius with anything electronic.

ACEE was held in a spacious shed in the grounds. It looked rickety on the outside but it opened into an Aladdin's cave. The interior was painted white, to make up for the fact that it had no windows. Blight liked to keep his inventions to himself. Every available space was taken up with computers and gadgetry – some old and quaint and some so new it looked as if they had never been used. The room smelled of oil and hot metal.

The Advanced CEE class was tiny: only Charlie, Agatha Quint and Jezebel Jackson, a Year Eleven who was head of De Bohun House and a master car thief, were considered competent enough to cope with the lessons. Each of the three students had their own personal workbench, littered with half-built contraptions, hand-drawn blueprints and their favourite tools.

Around the edges of the room were projects that one or other of them was working on, in various stages of completion. The bits of smashed-up cars were Jezebel Jackson's attempts at making a device that could boost a getaway car's speed by a thousand per cent in a single second. The acceleration was coming on well, but she was having problems with the braking.

There was a whole rack of handcuffs that Agatha Quint was working on. Some of them sent out electrical impulses that stunned the wearer; others emitted shrieks so high that they set every dog in Borage Bagpuize howling. She hadn't quite worked out a use for these yet, she said.

Next to Charlie's bench was the robot he was building, so large that it had to be stored in sections because it wouldn't fit in the room when it was assembled. He'd finished the legs and torso and was now working on the head. He called it Sid.

Charlie loved ACEE, but recently he'd begun to feel uncomfortable in the lessons. Agatha Quint had started using the classes to pick at him about his friendship with Milly.

'You know she drags you down, don't you?' she was saying, now. 'She's got no sense of humour – look at the way she reacted to poor Mr Huggins! And talk about bossy! Dump her and there'll be dozens of cool kids waiting to be friends with you.'

Charlie gave Agatha a vague smile and tried to ignore her. But sometimes he couldn't help but pay a *teensy* bit of attention to her. Not that he believed what she said, but now and then he'd leave the lesson wondering if life would be easier with more feloniously-minded friends.

The door opened and Herman Blight's handsome head appeared, smiling his too good to be true smile. 'Is he standing on a box?' Jezebel Jackson asked. 'He's got taller!'

Blight glided into the classroom. 'Taa dah!' he chanted. He was hovering about a foot above the floor. On his feet were what looked like tin foil high top trainers, fastened with Velcro. 'Apprentice Masterminds – you're witnessing a historic event. The first test flight of my hover boots. This day will go down in Felonious history. Watch this!'

He folded his arms and rose upwards, wobbling slightly, until his head was touching the ceiling. 'Think of all the ways these could be used,' Blight crowed. 'They'll be worth their weight in gold to any half indecent criminal!'

Charlie was gobsmacked. Jezebel Jackson's mouth was hanging open. 'Could you fix them to a car?' she asked, eyes glinting.

Agatha Quint was distracted. It seemed that she'd hardly registered Blight's amazing footwear. She had one hand in the air and the other was holding her mobile phone beneath the desk as she deleted a text. 'Sir, I've got to go. I've got a – a dental appointment. I'm being measured up for exploding braces,' she said.

Blight nodded his approval. 'Good Fabrication, Miss Quint. I'll be sure to mention it to Mr Borgia and tell him that I nearly believed you. Off you go!'

When the door had closed behind Agatha, Blight ducked beneath his desk and brought out a substantial box. 'I've been making hover boots in lots of different sizes. Fancy some fun?'

Charlie spent the rest of the lesson learning to fly around the room without crashing into the desks or splatting against the windows like a swatted fly. It wasn't easy. But it wasn't long before he was dodging furniture and zooming up to the ceiling.

It was a fun lesson and when the time came, Charlie removed the hover boots with reluctance. 'Thanks, Sir. They're brilliant. I wish I'd invented them!' He blurted the words out and then looked a bit embarrassed. But his spontaneous praise seemed to go down well and after Jezebel Jackson had managed to control her airsickness sufficiently to stagger out of the classroom, Blight patted Charlie on the back.

'I just wanted to say, Mr Partridge, that it's gratifying to find someone who truly appreciates my genius.' He beamed at Charlie. 'Someone with the ability to become a truly worthy apprentice. If you ever want to borrow some hover boots, you'll be very welcome.'

Charlie had a brainwave. He gave the teacher his most admiring smile. 'Actually, Sir, now that you mention it, I'd *love* to borrow some. Quite a few pairs. Do they come in extra small?'

CHAPTER TWENTY

'How did it all go?' Milly asked. She was sitting on Charlie's bed that evening, patting Gruffles, who'd been moping since Wolfie's capture.

Charlie gave a little smile. 'Not too bad. I've planted the false information and it's waiting to be discovered by the Brotherhood. And I've discovered something about Badpenny's family. Something interesting.' He paused.

'Go on!' Milly urged.

'Pecunia Badpenny isn't an only child, after all... She's got a baby brother. In fact–'

'Don't tell me. Twins – identical ones!'

'Got it in one. Ethereus and Cumulus. Current whereabouts unknown.'

'*Yes!*' Milly punched the air. 'I've said this before – you're a Hacking genius! Gabriel Huggins must really be Cumulus and Ethereus Badpenny, taking it in turns. That explains a lot. Huggins' amazing ability to change identity in about a second! Their eagerness to finish Badpenny's plan!'

Then Milly frowned. 'We've still got to find a way to

prove it, though. And we want to rescue Wolfie tomorrow. If the Brotherhood doesn't read the fake info, the plan won't work. Do you think they'll definitely find it tonight?'

Charlie tilted his head, considering. 'Yep, I can pretty well guarantee it. I've planted loads of hints about a secret website full of sensational information on Sir Bryon, that only the cleverest fans will be able to work out how to access. I've made it really easy for anyone who knows anything about Sir Bryon to access the fake site, too. There's a cryptic clue – the password is Sir Bryon's favourite dog treats. Get it?' His eyebrows lifted into his mop of hair.

He didn't have to wait long. 'Humbug – Sir Bryon's attack dog!' Milly said, triumphantly. 'But why will they look tonight?'

'We had a bit of luck there. Tomorrow is the anniversary of Sir Bryon's "untimely" death.' Charlie sketched air quotation marks. 'Every de Bohunite in the Felonious World will be trawling the web for new info about him.'

Milly nodded. 'That'll do it. Come on, we've got to raid the Disguise classroom. And the Science labs. Now we've got these hover boots, our disguises are going to be amazing!'

The Disguise classroom was locked, but Milly produced her set of Open-Sesame skeleton keys (her stocking present from her parents the previous Christmas) and opened it in a matter of seconds. 'Why did he bother locking it?' she asked, curling her lip. 'Even the Tiny Tyrants could open this!'

They entered quietly and Charlie aimed the light from his mobile around the classroom.

It looked as if Huggins had tried to impose some order on the mess that they'd seen the last time they were there.

The long racks of clothing had been arranged according to colour, starting with black, then greys, purples, blues, reds, browns, oranges, a wide array of greens, pinks and yellows, golds and silvers before ending with beige, cream and white.

The untidy pile of wigs that had been dumped on the floor had also been sorted according to colour, before being placed in plastic bins against one wall. In a tray on top of a long worktop were masses of pairs of glasses, some with their arms poking into the air like disabled spiders.

'Shall we look for some more dignified specs for Molesworthy?' Milly asked, with one eyebrow raised.

'Nope. After what he tried to do to Gruffles, I don't care how ridiculous he looks!'

'He'll be sorry. I promise. All of them will be... You're going to need a hat.' The teetering pile of hats had been tidied in to cardboard boxes. They'd been placed in front of the padlocked door that Milly had noticed during Huggins' introductory lesson.

Milly turned over a few hats before deciding on a tall one, a bit like an upside down flowerpot with a brim. 'That'll have to do! Let's hope William Proctor's not one of the Brotherhood. He'll probably say that your hat's historically inaccurate by three years!' She stuck it on Charlie's head. He looked in the mirror and snorted.

The next item she picked out was the tattiest sheepskin from a box of animal skins. Adding it to her booty, Milly pointed to the locked cupboard and said, 'Fancy finding out what "Huggins" is hiding in there?'

She didn't wait for an answer. Once again she plied her Open Sesame skeleton keys. But the lock remained stubbornly closed. 'Hmmm. Not so easy this time,' Milly commented. 'Must be a better lock. Whatever's in here, Huggins wants to make sure no one knows about it.' She rifled in one of her trouser pockets and produced an old-fashioned hairpin. 'This should do it. Good job I was paying attention In Lock Picking Club.'

Biting the tip of her tongue, she wiggled the hairpin into the lock and twisted it. All the while, Charlie was throwing worried looks at the door.

'Bingo!' Milly said, triumphantly.

They pulled open the door and found an old-fashioned coat rack. Hung with long robes. One of them was intricately embroidered with gallows and pistols and swords, in gold thread.

'There you go,' Milly said. 'Huggins is a Brother, too. That's two down – Molesworthy and Huggins – and three still to identify.'

In the bottom of the cupboard was a leather case with a label stuck to it. *VOICE CHANGERS. PROPERTY OF THE STAR WARS EXHIBITION. DO NOT REMOVE!* Milly opened it. Inside were dozens of thin black bands, each with a circular metallic disc attached in the middle and with sticky strips at both ends.

'So that's how they do it. We might be able to use these.' She grabbed a handful.

'We'd better relock the door and get on. We've got a lot to do tonight. And you've got to give me a flying lesson!' She headed for the racks of clothing.

'What about make up? Won't we need some?' Charlie pointed at a bench crammed with little pots and potions, in front of a long, horizontal mirror.

Milly shook her head. 'I've got something more drastic in mind!'

Five minutes later, the pair left the Deception and Disguise classroom, carrying bulging swag bags. They headed for the Science lab, after a brief excursion past the Assembly Hall.

By the time they reached the lab, with its long row of articulated skeletons all hanging like a still from a Halloween cartoon, their bags were straining at the seams.

'You know what we're looking for?' Milly whispered. She was opening drawers and cupboards, peering inside.

'I think so. Although what you want it for, I can't imagine.'

Gradually, they worked their way towards a dusty corner in which cracked beakers and melted Bunsen burners were kept before disposal. He opened the door of an ancient cupboard.

'Bingo.' He grabbed a glass jar with a screw-top lid and blew the dust off it. 'Messrs Blemysh and Boyle – Purveyors of the finest complexion aids to HM King George V,' he read, by the light from his mobile.

He turned the jar towards the window for a little extra light. 'Urgh. It's gone green. Luminous green. Are you sure about this?'

Milly came to stand behind him. She took the jar, unscrewed the lid, smelt the contents and then stuck one finger in. It came out an unearthly, glowing shade of lime.

'Perfect,' she nodded with satisfaction. 'Let's take lots. We going to need it.'

CHAPTER TWENTY-ONE

The following day began with the news that Agatha Quint had disappeared. No one had seen her since she'd excused herself from the previous day's ACEE lesson. Ms Martinet announced her absence in Assembly, then organised groups to search the school and grounds.

'I'm convinced that she's still on the premises,' the Head Teacher said glaring around as if she suspected everyone of helping Agatha to hide herself away. 'Her uniform is missing. So she must still be wearing it. She knows better than to leave the school grounds in it.'

Milly nodded. That made sense. No one, not even someone running away from the school, would risk being seen outside Blaggard's in their school uniform. The penalty for doing so – Ms Martinet's wrath – was too horrible to contemplate.

Lessons were suspended while the search was conducted, which was inconvenient for Charlie, who had to pretend that he suddenly felt unwell so that he could leave the Assembly Hall and retrieve Gruffles from the woods, before the searchers stumbled across him. 'It's one thing catching a glimpse of a ghostly hound as you creep through the woods, when you're not really meant to be there,' he'd explained to Milly, afterwards. 'It's a different thing altogether to have big groups of Blaggardians combing the woods and scaring him. His cover would be blown in no time!'

The search was unsuccessful and lessons recommenced before lunchtime.

For Milly and Charlie, the day stretched ahead endlessly. 'Why don't we go now? Get it over with?' Charlie fretted as they waited in the lunch queue. 'The waiting is killing me.'

Milly shook her head. 'I know it's hard. I don't know how I'm going to eat anything. That's assuming there's any food left to eat, by the time we get to the front of the queue.' She sidestepped to avoid a pair of low-flying radishes, artistically cut into flower shapes. 'But it'll be much more convincing at night. And I need some more practice with the hover boots. We're going to need every bit of luck we can get to do this right.'

Afternoon lessons were torture. In Disguise and Deception, the pair could barely look at Gabriel Huggins. He seemed to be surprised that they weren't more enthusiastic when, after a quick demonstration, it was their turn to practice their skills in sheep impersonation.

There was an awkward moment when Huggins was distributing sheepskins to the class, and he discovered that he was one short. 'Oh dear,' he whispered. 'I've mislaid one.' He fussed around looking for it for a minute or two. 'Never mind, Mr Proctor. You can be a wolf instead!' He handed William a shaggy wolf skin.

The final lesson of the afternoon was Defiance and Discourtesy, and by the time it came around, both Milly and Charlie were close to losing their cool. The lesson began in the usual way, with Miss Vipond picking on anyone who caught her eye.

Charlie was one of her regular targets. 'You. Partridge. When are you going to stop acting like a little girl and think up some original insults for me? ' she snarled at him.

Charlie had had enough. He looked her up and down. 'Tell you what, Miss. I'll think up some original insults when you stop dressing like you're trying to disguise yourself as a sack of potatoes. Small, shrivelled, unappetising potatoes,' he retorted, emphasising each insult. Then his cheeks flamed and his hand flew to his mouth.

Miss Vipond blinked and took a step backwards. 'Well,' she said. 'Small, shrivelled potatoes. Very good. Take twenty house points. And if you want to reach your next birthday, never say that to me again!'

-oOo-

During dinner Milly sneaked out of the dining hall and along to the Junior Common Room, where she picked the lock of the Sally Masters display case.

She was removing her heroine's tricorn hat and long, caped coat when she heard Mrs Christie's heavy tread, outside the room. Quickly, Milly put the coat back on its stand, climbed inside it and pulled the display case door until it was nearly closed. She held her breath. Through one of the coat's buttonholes, she saw Mrs Christie peering into the room. The Boarding Mistress moved on, leaving

Milly thanking the stars that she was small. She bundled her booty into a ball and hurried back to her room.

Some time later she got a text from Charlie: '*R u coming down?*'

'*On my way,*' she texted back. She collected everything she needed and two minutes later she was knocking on Charlie's door.

The door opened a little and his anxious face appeared. 'This is mad,' he blurted, opening the door wider.

Milly entered his room and was brought up short by a disturbing sight. A zombie creature seemed to have crawled out of some dank tomb and was sitting on Charlie's floor. Scattered over its dripping green flesh were lumps of its lank, woolly coat, presumably the last bits to drop off as it decomposed. Its eyes were black-rimmed and it stank of corruption.

'Hello Gruffles,' Milly said. 'You look revolting. And you smell worse.' She grinned at Charlie. 'Well done. That's disgusting, even for Gruffles.'

Gruffles wagged his tail and gave a little yip. But the sound came out as a high-pitched, human voice. 'Roof!' he exclaimed.

Gruffles jumped back from the sound of his own voice. Timidly, he tried a little bark. This time it came out as: 'Beef!'

Milly listened, open-mouthed. 'Charlie, that's brilliant. You managed to adjust the voice changer, then. Does he mind wearing it?'

Charlie reached out to stroke his dog, touched the goo that besmeared him and changed his mind. 'He's not a fan,' he said. 'But I don't think he's exactly relishing any part of his disguise. He hates the hover boots. I've taken them off him until we're outside.'

'He'll get used to them. The Blemysh and Boyle spot cream makes wonderful decomposing flesh. I told you it wasn't toxic! We'd better get ready, too.' She headed for Charlie's little bathroom, but turned back with her hand on the door handle. 'I've got to ask – how did you make Gruffles smell so disgusting? It's about a million times worse than his own smell. I didn't think it was possible!'

'I had a brainwave,' Charlie glowed with pride. 'I pinched Jet Mannington's mud-wrestling kit and got Gruffles to roll around in it. I reckon Jet only washes it once a year. The socks...' he rolled his eyes and fanned the air in front of his nose.

'Brilliant,' Milly grinned.

Twenty minutes later, the number of hideous beings in Charlie's room had increased to three. As well as the hell-hound, there was a zombie Findlay Foggarty in mud-stained tatters, and an undead Sally Masters, so shrivelled and shrunken by centuries in the tomb that her long coat dragged on the ground behind her.

'Hope I don't trip over this coat,' Milly said. 'We'll be floating when we meet the Brothers. That'll help.' She looked around Charlie's room. 'You look horrible. Findlay Foggarty's death mask was a master touch, especially now it's dripping with luminous cream! Did you manage to find a spade? You can't be a body snatcher without a spade.'

Charlie nodded. 'Yep. It's waiting in the woods. I was going to go to Growing Paynes – you know, the garden centre in Borage Bagpuize – to buy one. But I realised it would be shiny and new and unzombie-like so I pinched one from the gardener's shed instead. It's filthy. I wouldn't be surprised if it actually *was* Findlay Foggarty's spade. It looks old enough!'

'Cool. I reckon we're ready. We just need to give the school a bit more time to settle down...'

They waited, trying not to drip Blemysh and Boyle goo onto Charlie's bed. Gruffles was staying absolutely still for once, although whether this was because he could sense danger, or just the discomfort of being dressed like a rotting zombie, Milly couldn't tell.

Charlie opened his laptop and started hacking. *That'll calm him down*, Milly thought. She peered over Charlie's shoulder for a few minutes, then got bored and reached for her bag. In the bottom there were the big glass dice she'd bought from WORNOUT.

She pulled them out, blowing the dust off them. Inside the glass were odd swirls that seemed to shimmer and twist as she watched them. The writing on them was faded almost to the point of being illegible. She moved them around in her hands. They felt warm and comforting. She rolled them on the floor, bending close to decipher the words on them.

On one of the dice, the writing was so faded that it was impossible to work out. *Wonder what it said? A single word, quite long. A name?*

She picked up one of the other dice and squinted at it. G-A-B-R. The rest of the letters were rubbed beyond recognition. *Gabriel? What about the other one?* The writing on this one was a bit easier to read. H-U-G-G-I-N-S. *Huggins! Gabriel Huggins!*

There seemed to be something else on scratched into the corner of one of the dice. Milly held it up to the light and squinted.

'Charlie,' Milly tried to keep the excitement out of her voice. 'It looks like I've accidentally bought some Orcadian Naming Dice. They're coming up with the name Gabriel Huggins!'

Charlie's mouth dropped open.

'Just look at in this corner, will you?' Milly passed the dice to her friend. 'And tell me if it says what I think it says.'

He pushed his hair away from his eyes and held the dice up. It took him a few seconds to work out the tiny writing. *'Property of Ethereus Badpenny'*, he read. He turned to look at Milly with wide eyes. 'Do you remember "Huggins" saying that he'd lost his Naming Dice? And the man in the junk shop telling us that he bought these from a pair of twins? This is it. Proof that Huggins is a Badpenny!'

CHAPTER TWENTY-TWO

H alf an hour later, they emerged from the secret tunnel that led from behind the stuffed corpse of Sir Bryon de Bohun in the Assembly Hall, and out into Blaggard's woods.

They made a short detour to collect Charlie's spade and, finding an old wheelbarrow that the gardener had left, cleared the rubbish off it and took that, too. Then they set off to confront the Brotherhood. The wheelbarrow slowed down their journey, as they had to manoeuvre it around trees and over lumps in the ground. But Milly assured Charlie that it would be worth the effort. As they got closer to the sewage room, they fell quiet.

All too soon they reached their destination. They stood still, listening to the silence that seemed to press in around them. It was shattered when a little gust of wind threw some rustling leaves into their path and an owl hooted, close by. 'That owl doesn't need a voice changer to call us twits,' Charlie commented.

'We're not twits,' Milly said, firmly. 'This is for Wolfie,

who saved our lives not long ago. Let's hide the wheelbarrow and disguise our hover boots and get them on. And the voice changers. I'll do the talking... Everyone reeaady?' The final word was a long, drawn-out moan, as she switched on her voice changer.

Charlie nodded.

'Brimstone,' Milly called.

The door slid open and they floated inside.

-oOo-

The lights were flaring, illuminating an eerie scene.

All five Brothers were there. Four were gathered around the black-draped table. Their shadows spiked away from them and across the floor like black stalactites. The fifth – the Brother Superior – was standing on top of the table. His hands were smeared with red.

Milly and Charlie were in time to see him hurl a rubber chicken to the ground and to hear him say, '–the Gallows Dance!'

He began to move. He shuffled his feet. His body jerked spasmodically. His arms were rigid and his hands convulsed. His head seemed to be stuck out at an unnatural angle. It wasn't attractive.

Milly's jaw dropped. *He's pretending that he's being hanged!*

The other Brothers swayed and chanted in their weird, alien voices:

Brimstone, Grimstone, Bad and Bold,

Evil weevil, Lust for Gold...

Milly, Charlie and Gruffles glided forward. The Brothers

were so wrapped up in their ceremony that no one noticed the new arrivals. At least, not at first. But as the dance reached its climax, a discordant scraping sound made the worshippers halt and swivel towards the door. They gasped.

Milly tried to imagine what they were seeing: three nightmare creatures bearing down on them. 'Sally Masters' was in the lead, drifting noiselessly through the air three feet above the ground. Beneath her tricorn hat, her face glowed an eerie, patchy green. Next came 'Findlay Foggarty', gliding a little closer to the ground but still well above it. His decaying face looked rigid and disdainful. His filthy spade was dragging along one wall, throwing sparks into the air.

Bringing up the rear and flying in erratic circles, sometimes upright, sometimes tilting at an angle, was a zombie hound. From his gaping jaws, a human word sometimes emerged. 'Beef,' he moaned.

The Brother Superior looked like a statue. He was frozen in the middle of the table, head still cocked at an unnatural angle. He struggled to find his voice. 'W–who? ... what...?' he stammered, in his strange voice.

'Why 'ave you disturbed us?' Milly asked, in the kind of rural accent that she thought Sally Masters would have had. 'We were quite comfortable, bein' dead. But all your worshippin' and sacrificin' has woken us up.'

'Disturbed your rest?' Superior said. 'Who are you? *Were* you?'

'Who are *you?*' Milly retorted, drifting round the group of Brothers and assessing them. Charlie and Gruffles followed close behind in a creepy little procession.

'We're the Brotherhood of Brimstone. We worship Sir Bryon de Bohun and plan horrible things for Blaggardians and Dependables,' Superior said.

'Bryon? My Bryon? No wonder our eternal rest has been disturbed!' Milly said, trying her hardest to sound peeved. And rural. And weird.

One of the Brothers – the one in the dark green robe – found his voice. '*Your* Bryon? So it's true? I found some new information last night on a secret website. It said that Sir Bryon's birth certificate had been discovered. And that his mother was Blunderbuss Sally!'

Milly didn't need to look at Charlie to know that he was trying to hide a satisfied smile.

'DON'T call me that!' Milly's voice rose. She loomed over the brother in green. 'It's not respectful.'

The Brother backed away. Suddenly, the zombie hound zoomed up to the ceiling. 'Half!' it wailed.

Hellfire, hope he doesn't crash. That would be hard to explain, Milly thought. Thankfully, Gruffles mastered himself in time. He stopped in mid-air, spun around a few times and then plummeted back to his original place. A lump of his sheepskin fell off. Milly kicked it under the table.

The four lesser Brothers drew closer together. 'Half of what? *Wheeb!* What does it mean? Why can it speak?' the one in red asked.

'Why not?' Milly retorted. 'In the afterlife, anythin's possible. He hasn't mastered the meanin's of words yet. But it's early days, in ghost years. He's Humbug, my Bryon's pet. He's heard there's an imposter imitatin' him, so he's come back to tear his throat out. Haven't you, Humbug?'

She glanced behind her. Now Gruffles seemed to be dozing off in mid-air. Charlie gave him a furtive poke in the ribs. Startled, the dog shrieked, 'Roof!' and jetted into one of the table legs.

While the Brothers were watching 'Humbug', Milly gave Charlie a tiny nod. He drifted around the corner, spade in hand, searching for Wolfie.

Superior dragged his attention back to Milly. 'It's an honour to meet Sir Bryon's mother. And his –?' There was a question in Superior's voice as he looked after Charlie's mouldy back.

'His brother. Well, half-brother, if oim bein' honest. Findlay Foggarty. He went into a different line o' felony. He was very successful for a bit, but his career came to a nasty end...' Milly jerked her neck and poked her tongue out of the corner of her mouth. 'When we saw your gallows dance, we thought you was re-enactin' Findlay's end. Bryon didn't die on the gallows, young man.'

'I know,' it was the Brother in brown who answered. He sounded defensive. 'But – look – it's on this cloth.' He pointed to the embroidered sets of gallows on the black blanket covering the table. 'We've proved that it belonged to Sir Bryon. That's why we use it in our ceremonies!'

'Belonged to him? 'Course it belonged to him. It were 'is cot blanket. He loved to sleep in it, suckin' his little pink thumb. When he got a bit older, he used to wrap his teddies in it,' Milly improvised, starting to enjoy herself. 'His favourite was called Cap'n Fluffy.'

'*Cot blanket?*' the Brother in brown looked disgusted. '*Teddies? Fluffy?*'

Milly sent him a look of spectral impatience. 'D'you always repeat everything? It's annoyin',' she said. 'He wasn't at all like his legend. He weren't that evil. Or 'andsome. The way his body looks,' she pointed at the grotesque replica – 'that's not bad stuffing. He really did have wonky eyes. He were brilliant with make-up, though...'

'*Make-up?*' the Brother in brown sounded scandalised.

'You're doin' it again. Repeatin' everything. Yes he wore make up. And he always wore that lumpy diamond o' his – so that people would be too busy staring at it to notice that he weren't that handsome. He made up Humbug, too, to make him look more like 'is fearsome portrait.'

'*Dog make up?*' Inferior repeated, incredulously.

'He was a wizard with a mascara wand,' Milly improvised. She was watching for Charlie to reappear around the corner.

When he did appear, there was something about his slumped shoulders that warned Milly that she wasn't going to like what she saw.

CHAPTER TWENTY-THREE

Milly put her hands up to the sides of her forehead and rubbed it with her glowing fingertips. 'I'm gettin' some ghostly vibes. Stay where you are. I need to communicate with Findlay, in a mysterious way.'

She floated after Charlie, who had disappeared back round the corner. Gruffles tailed after her. He was having trouble with his hover boots again and was upside down now, grumbling to himself.

And then Milly saw a terrible sight.

We're too late, she thought, dully.

Wolfie was on lying on the floor, still dormant. But he was changed. Horribly changed. His blunt face had been drawn out into a sharp, elongated spiral, similar to the mole Milly had doodled in Betrayal class. The long probes on either side of his head, that looked so much like floppy dog ears, had been torn off and were lying on the ground next to him. His many tails had been discarded too, and had been replaced with a single upright metal antenna, bristling with chainsaw teeth. Next to the inert monster, waiting to be attached, were two giant metal scoops, riveted onto long arms.

The worst things were his eyes. Wolfie's had been huge and they danced with mischief and lights that changed colour, according to his mood. Now they were just tiny pinpricks, dead and black.

Gruffles had finally regained control of his hover boots. He landed next to Wolfie and nosed his friend's cold body. 'Howwww?' he wailed. *How indeed,* Milly thought, her body cold with anger.

'I'm still working on a way of attaching the scoops,' an alien voice said, behind them. 'I'm Maggot, by the way, the Brother Superior's apprentice. What do you think of my work? I know you told us to stay around the corner, but I couldn't wait to show you.'

'It's – astonishin',' Milly managed. 'You deserve a special reward for doing this. And 'ere it is.' Her voice dropped. 'My ghostly contacts have dropped me a hint that Ms Martinet has just deposited a mountain o' money in the school safe. But it's only there tonight. Tomorrow it's goin' to be moved to a secret place. Why don't you...?'

Maggot hesitated, as if he was considering his options. 'Do the other Brothers know about the money?' he asked, casually.

'Not yet. We'll go and tell them, shall we?' This was Charlie. *Thank Hades for his voice changer,* Milly thought. *Even with it on, I can hear the upset in his voice.*

'No! No, I'll tell them later,' Maggot spluttered. 'I've, er, got to go now. Don't bother mentioning the money, will you? They're pretty busy at the moment.'

Maggot scurried round the corner. Milly and Charlie could hear him making hurried excuses to the other Brothers. 'I've got to make a move now. I need to steal a lot of – stuff from the CEE classroom. To finish building the Mole. I won't be long...'

There was the sound of quick footsteps; then Milly and Charlie heard the word 'Brimstone'. The door opened, then closed again.

'What shall we do, Mills?' Charlie whispered. 'They've murdered Wolfie!' Milly saw his hands shaking. Briefly, she took them between her own.

'We're going to get him out of here, for starters,' she promised. 'Before they do anything else to him. Let's pick up his ears and tails and hide them in our clothes. I'll try talking our way out, but if it doesn't work, you've got your spade. And Gruffles has his teeth. I'll improvise.'

A minute later, the three zombies drifted back around the corner to confront the Brotherhood.

'What do you think?' Superior asked. 'I can't wait to set him loose on the Dependable world. I was thinking of getting him to destroy the Houses of Parliament first, to save on travel costs, but now I'm veering towards the Taj Mahal. I've always hated it. A testament to *love*...' He shook his head. 'The Mole's new sonic sabre will reduce it to rubble in about ten seconds, once he's burrowed underneath it!'

Milly stopped dead. 'Mole? It be a *mole?* I hadn't realised!'

'Of course it's a mole. An evil mole. What did you think it was?' The Brother in the red robe asked.

Milly hesitated. 'I thought it were a hamster. I were a bit surprised. Not the most evil creatures, hamsters.' *As the*

Crumleians found out, with the Marquis of Bimblethorpe, Milly thought, remembering William Proctor's story about Crumley's search for an evil animal.

'A *hamster?*' Superior's voice changer couldn't hide the fact that he was offended. 'What part of it looks like a hamster?'

'All of it,' Charlie chipped in. 'And I don't think our Bryon would have liked it. His image was always important to him. He won't want Dependables thinking of him as the tyrant who inspired a giant hamster. It's insulting.'

Well done, Charlie, Milly thought, *that's a great touch.*

Gruffles seemed to agree. 'Rough,' he announced, suddenly.

There was a disconcerted grumbling among the Brotherhood. It sounded as if a group of aliens had come a long way for an intergalactic party, and then when they got there, they weren't allowed in.

'I don't think it's remotely hamstery,' Superior riposted, after thoroughly inspecting the Wolf, one of his hands raised to his invisible chin.

Eureka! I've remembered who uses that gesture! Milly put the thought to the back of her mind until it was safe to process it. She gave the Wolf a quick, doubtful examination. 'It be bit dark back there. Bring it in here, where the light be better, and we'll have another peek.'

The Brother in green put his hands on his hips. 'Why don't you go and get it?' he asked.

'Us?' Charlie sounded outraged. 'We're not getting it. We're ancient zombies! That's a job for inferiors. If that apprentice – Maggot – was here, I'd say get him to do it, but he's gone now, so it's down to you.'

'–Of course,' Milly took over, 'if you'd rather just dump the hamst–, er, Mole, and think of a more 'orrible way of celebrating my Bryon, that's fine...'

Superior shoved Posterior and Inferior. 'You two, go and get it. And be careful. It's heavy.'

The Brothers in brown and red stomped away, looking back over their shoulders as they went. Their faces were hidden, but Milly assumed that they were throwing dirty looks at Superior.

A minute later they reappeared, struggling with Wolfie. As soon as they rounded the corner, they dumped their burden on the floor and stood up straight.

Milly and Charlie exchanged a look of alarm. They'd hoped that Wolfie would end up much nearer to the door. It would make their task a lot easier. Milly drifted over to the inert metal figure. She made a show of peering at it.

'No good,' she said. 'Still too dark. Can't you put it over there where's there's more light?' She lifted a ghostly hand and pointed towards the door.

Moaning alien moans, the pair picked Wolfie up again and staggered towards the door. They put him down with a clatter.

'Happy now?' the Brother in brown asked.

Milly ignored the question and glided over to Wolfie. 'Findlay, come and have a look,' she called to Charlie. He leaned his spade against the wall and followed her.

The pair floated to the ground, to examine Wolfie. The Brothers had drawn closer too, and were watching them like wary hawks. Private talk was impossible. Milly flashed her eyes at Charlie. He gave a tiny nod. They straightened up.

'No, I'm still not convinced,' Milly said. 'How 'bout you, Findlay?'

Charlie shook his head. 'No. To me, it's one hundred per cent hamster. All it needs is a plastic wheel and a peanut to nibble. What shall we do with it, M–' he stopped himself just in time. '–Mumsy?'

Milly suppressed a snort at the thought of being Charlie's mum. 'I think we should take it away. Do some work on it. Maybe get a second opinion from some of t'other zombie folk. We'll have it back in a day or two...'

She grabbed one end of the metal creature. Charlie took the other. They levitated, wobbling a little under the weight. But it was only a metre or so to the door.

Gruffles had been hovering anxiously around his friend. Suddenly, he realised that he had an itch under his chin. It seemed that he'd forgotten that he wasn't on terra firma and he tried to extend one of his back legs for a good scratch. He tipped upside down like a capsizing canoe. 'Cress!' he exclaimed, surprised.

In the ensuing scrumble, two of his hover boots fell off. Although Milly and Charlie had covered the exteriors of the boots with Blemysh and Boyle cream, their insides were still silvery and reasonably clean. They didn't look remotely zombie-like.

The boots that had fallen off had both been on Gruffles' left-hand side. Without them, that side of him dropped to the ground, although his right side was still levitated. He looked like he was performing a canine can-can. 'Yikes,' he yipped, in consternation.

It was at that moment that the Brothers finally realised they were being duped. They launched into action.

'They're not zombies! They're stealing the Mole. Kill them!' Superior yelled. He bore down on Milly, pulling his long, curved dagger from his robe.

CHAPTER TWENTY-FOUR

Milly and Charlie dropped Wolfie and spun to face their enemies. 'Gruffles, ATTACK!' Charlie yelled. Gruffles looked at Charlie with uncertainty on his green face. 'Steeew?' he asked, doubtfully.

'It's your voice. He's not sure it's you. Take your voice changer off,' Milly shouted. She dodged a killer blow from Superior and flew past the outstretched arms of Posterior with reasonable deftness.

Charlie ripped the voice changer away from his throat. 'Gruffles – ATTACK!' he yelled again.

Now that he had confirmation that Charlie actually *wanted* him to bite the horrible people who'd done such awful things to Wolfie, Gruffles threw himself into his task with gusto, roaring *'BEEF! ROOF! HALF!'*

He hurled himself onto Inferior's back, just as the Brother was reaching for Charlie's legs. The dog dug his teeth deep into the meat at the top of Inferior's right arm. Inferior gave a wail and dropped into a ball on the floor, cradling his wound and moaning.

Charlie bent over and glared at him. 'We know it's you, Molesworthy. Stay out of this. For your own good. Next time, it won't be your arm he goes for.'

Molesworthy looked up into Charlie's face. 'Who are you?' he whispered.

Charlie didn't bother replying.

Anterior had been watching and waiting. Now he made his move. He lunged for possession of the spade that Charlie had just picked up again and a tug of war began, with the big table in between them.

Milly had been driven against a wall between Superior, with his wickedly curving knife, and Posterior, who seemed to be hanging back just a bit, for some reason. Gruffles was closer to Posterior. He chomped his teeth into the Brother's red robe and pulled backwards. There was a long tearing sound. A big patch of the robe came away in Gruffles' mouth, revealing a flash of beige underneath. The dog shot backwards, bashing into the wall.

Milly saw a possible escape route. Posterior was distracted, hurriedly trying to cover his everyday clothes. Milly dashed past him, heading for the giant aerosols.

She grabbed the nearest one, whipped round and aimed it at Superior, who was bearing down on her, knife raised.

'Drop it, or this goes off in your face,' she spat.

Superior hesitated. Then he took a step closer. Milly aimed a shot of PONG-O-RAMA at him. He stopped, gagging. Milly did too, a little, but Superior got the brunt of it. He bent double and clamped one hand over his nose.

'OK. OK,' he gulped. He dropped his knife onto the floor.

Milly looked at Posterior who was crouching slightly,

ready to attack. 'Stand up. Kick that knife away, or you'll get this,' Milly ordered. Posterior paused for a moment. Milly aimed a tiny squirt at him. His hands shot into the air.

Anterior was still struggling with Charlie for possession of the spade, but seeing his brethren defeated, he dropped his end of it. Inferior was still curled up on the floor, moaning about the blood he'd lost.

'So, what now?' Superior asked.

'We're taking the Wolf,' Milly replied. 'If you try and stop us, you get this – a massive dose this time. Enough to make you smell like sewage for the rest of your lives. You'll be dreaming of sewage. Your friends will desert you because you'll stink. That's assuming you've got any friends. And we'll set the dog on you, too. He hates you for what you've done to the Wolf.'

She edged up to Wolfie, taking care not to turn her back on the Brothers, and picked up one end of the metal dog. Charlie picked up the other. He raised his eyebrows. Milly gave him a nod.

'Brimstone,' Charlie called.

Just before they slipped out into the night, Milly whipped round and sprayed a long, choking plume of PONG-O-RAMA into the room. The door slammed behind them, sealing the stink inside. Her last glimpse of the Brothers was of them hanging onto the walls, spewing onto the floor.

'That'll hold them up for a bit,' she said, mopping her smarting eyes.

Charlie saw the length of rusty metal that he'd used to lever open the door on his first visit to the Sewage Room.

He picked it up and wedged it firmly under the bottom of the door. 'And that'll give us a few more minutes,' he said.

Milly grinned. 'Nice one!'

They bundled Wolfie into the wheelbarrow and, with Gruffles anxiously watching over his friend, hurried away.

-oOo-

They left Wolfie and their disguises in the CEE classroom.

'I'm going to ask Mr Blight for help in changing Wolfie back,' Charlie said. Milly opened her mouth to protest. He held up one hand to stop her.

'No, I know you won't like it, but it's the only way. I can't put him back together alone. I need some help,' Charlie assured her. 'Trust me. For once.'

Milly gave him a long look, thinking hard. *I do trust him. Of course I do. It's just that it's hard, sometimes, to let someone else take control.*

'OK,' she said. 'Let's go and get Blight.

They made a quick detour to leave Gruffles in Charlie's room, and to wipe off the worst of the Blemysh and Boyle. Then they set off for Mr Blight's little house, which was one of several dotted just beyond Blaggard's main building.

Before they'd even set foot outside, a tall figure loomed silently up out of the shadows in front of them.

'Miss Dillane. Mr Partridge. I've been looking for you,' Ms Martinet said. 'I've got something interesting to show you. Come with me.'

It wasn't a request. Milly raised her eyebrows at the note of excitement in the Head Teacher's voice.

CHAPTER TWENTY-FIVE

Ms Martinet led them to her office and flicked on the light.

Across the room Milly saw that the black pit was once again gaping in front of the safe. From deep inside it, an alien voice was feebly calling for help.

YES! Milly thought. *Revenge for Wolfie.*

'I'm *ab-so-lutely* delighted to say that we've snared a robber. Shall we see who it is, or shall I just press Vlad's left eye and have done with it?' Ms Martinet purred.

'I think I know who it is, Miss,' Milly replied. 'At least, I know one of his identities. He calls himself Maggot. He's part of a secret group that's meeting in the school grounds. They've resurrected the Brotherhood of Brimstone and pinched Sir Bryon's Brain. I told him there was a lot of new cash in your safe. I was pretty sure he wouldn't be able to resist stealing it.'

Ms Martinet looked hopeful. 'Have you retrieved the Brain?'

Milly shook her head. 'Not yet. We don't know where it is at the moment, but we're working on it.'

'I wonder if this traitor knows?' Ms Martinet called into the pit: 'You – Maggot – tell me where the Brain is, and I won't kill you.'

'I can't!' Maggot's voice was an alien wail of distress. 'I don't know. They wouldn't tell me. I'm only the apprentice!'

'In that case, I think that the eye-pressing option really does sound like the best solution. We'd better get some overalls on – there'll be lots of blood flying around.'

She pulled open a drawer in her huge desk. Inside, Milly saw several pairs of black overalls, neatly folded. 'I've got some ready,' Ms Martinet smiled.

'Wait!' the alien voice sounded panicked now. 'Wait. Ms Martinet. Please.'

There was a ripping sound, which Milly realised was Maggot removing his voice changer.

'Please, Miss,' a female voice called from the pit. 'It's me. Agatha Quint. I'm really sorry. I'll resign from the Brotherhood immediately. Please don't kill me.'

-oOo-

After persuading Ms Martinet that pressing Vlad the Emailer's left eye to obliterate Agatha in spectacular style would create more problems than it solved, Milly and Charlie hurried to Herman Blight's house and rapped on his door.

He clearly hadn't been expecting company. He opened the door wearing a silk smoking jacket. A hairnet was ensuring that his messed-up hair didn't get tidier as he slept.

Doing his best not to stare at the hairnet, Charlie explained why they were there.

Blight gave a nod. 'I'm not surprised,' he said. 'I spotted the Wolf's potential immediately, and if I hadn't given up active criminality for the gentle life of a Blaggardian teacher, I'd have been tempted to have a go at evilising him myself.'

He'd gone into his bedroom to put on some overalls and was speaking through the door. He hesitated for a second. 'I don't suppose you'd let me have a little play with him?' he asked, in a wheedling voice. 'Just for fun's sake? I'd love to see what I could do with him. I've even drawn up a few blueprints–'

'NO!' Milly and Charlie shouted, in unison.

'*OK*, OK. Just a thought... ' He strode out of his bedroom in immaculate white overalls and threw his hairnet onto the floor.

'Let's get down to business.'

-oOo-

After a sleepless night working on Wolfie, Milly and Charlie dragged themselves into Assembly the following morning, wondering what Ms Martinet would have to say about the previous night's events.

The Head Teacher was even terser than usual. She'd been prowling backwards and forwards across the stage as they filed into their places, but as soon as the last Blaggardian bum had made contact with a seat, she stopped stalking and began to speak.

'Good morning, tyrants of tomorrow. A quick, blunt message is all I have for you today. The school is on lock down. No one gets in. No one gets out. Until Founders' Day. The reason is this: some ill-advised Blaggardians – staff *and* students – have resurrected an infamous secret society and are plotting against the school. If they were just cooking up plots against Dependables, I'd turn a blind eye. But this is *ab-so-lutely* UNACCEPTABLE!' She glared around.

'Two of those involved – a student and a teacher – have been apprehended and are being held somewhere safe. They're refusing to spill the beans about the others at the moment, but I'm sure I can change that, when I have a moment.' She gave a grim smile and flexed her fingers.

Every Blaggardian head except Milly's and Charlie's began scanning the line of teachers, to see who was missing.

'It seems that these ill-advised felons may attempt to hunt down certain Blaggardians who are offering me some private assistance.' Ms Martinet's eyes swept the room, meeting Milly's for a fraction of a second.

'Those Blaggardians are under my personal protection. All of the school's *stupendous* security measures will be deployed to keep them safe. You won't see those measures, but I give you my word as a master felon that they will be there and they are lethal.'

'So–,' she leapt from the stage and stalked through the rows of seats, 'leave those students ALONE. Or you will be very sorry. VERY. Now go about your business. And remember – today could be the day that Dr X arrives to inspect us. Be on your worst behaviour!'

She dismissed the whole school with a wave of her hand and departed, leaving the double doors swinging in her wake.

-oOo-

Milly and Charlie skipped their lessons that day to continue their work on Wolfie.

'Mr Blight won't mind,' Charlie said, on their way back to the ACEE room. 'He doesn't have any CEE lessons today, so he won't need the classroom. As for our other lessons, it's only Disguise and Deception, followed by Betrayal for you and Hacking for me. After lunch it's Defiance and Discourtesy, so we'll annoy Miss Vipond if we're not there, but when you think about it, that's the whole point of her lesson!'

They were heading down one of the long corridors that branched off from Reception, past a row of portraits of long-dead Head Teachers. Charlie fell silent for a few seconds and then said: 'I've got this weird feeling that we're being watched.'

'Me too,' Milly replied. They looked around. There was no one in sight. Charlie shrugged and they moved off again. But the uncomfortable feeling that eyes were boring into them continued. They stopped again. Peered around again.

'Look!' Milly pointed at the painting of Jericho Smithers, Headmaster for about ten days in 1722. Smithers' eyes were darting around everywhere. Charlie scrutinised the painting with an expert eye. 'Electronic movement detectors. They must feed back to a control room. I wonder where that is?'

'Another of Ms Martinet's secret improvements, I suppose,' Milly said, waving. 'Hi Ms Martinet! It's nice to know we're being protected.'

They turned to resume their walk, but had only gone a pace or two before Ms Martinet's disembodied voice boomed out, making them jump. 'You could at least pretend that you hadn't spotted the hidden camera. We'll never catch the Brotherhood if you point out every little trap I've set for them!'

'Sorry, Miss,' Charlie said. But it didn't stop him nudging Milly to silently indicate every hidden camera and, once outside, every mini drone disguised as a bird, as they made their way back to the ACEE classroom.

It was a long, difficult day. Even with Herman Blight popping in to offer advice and practical help, trying to mend Wolfie was the hardest thing Charlie had ever done. He'd equipped himself with some high-definition magnifying specs to help him with the most intricate restoration, but even so it wasn't long before his head was pounding and his hands were shaking.

'The problem is that whoever converted him was a clumsy amateur with no more finesse than a smash and grabber in baseball mitts in an egg factory,' Blight had said, with an angry shake of his head. 'If you or I, Mr Partridge, had undertaken this task, we'd have approached it with the delicacy it deserves.' He picked up Wolfie's severed ear probes and brandished them. 'Look at this! *Ripped* away and discarded like a pair of holey socks. Who did this?'

Charlie threw Milly a glance of enquiry. She nodded.

'Actually, sir, it was Agatha Quint,' Charlie said.

'Really? I'm not surprised,' Blight said. 'I never thought that Agatha should be in Advanced CEE. She was clearly out of her depth. Did you *see* the mess she made when she tried to combine an electric toothbrush with a handheld hoover? h

Then he flitted off again, promising to return when he could. Just before he reached the door, he turned and said, 'By the way, Mr Partridge, you're doing a brilliant job, especially with some of those modifications you've come up with. I hate to admit it, but I couldn't do it better myself. *Possibly* I couldn't do as well, although it would be a close thing, obviously...'

Charlie gave a tiny smile and returned to his task. With painstaking care he detached the horrible pointed snout from Wolfie's face. That made him look a bit better. Then he removed the metal tail, with its chainsaw teeth. That helped, too. But Wolfie was still dormant. *I won't use the word 'dead',* Charlie thought to himself. *I refuse to use that word.*

'Let's get his ears reattached,' Charlie said mournfully, after staring at the lifeless body on his bench. 'He'll have one ear shorter than the other from now on.'

'He won't mind that,' Milly reassured him. 'He'll think it's funny.'

'Yes. Yes, he will. We'll tease him about it.' What Charlie thought, but what didn't say, was: *But only if I can put him back together properly. It's not just the stuff on the outside. Agatha's mangled his insides, too. I've done my best, but I just don't know if it'll work.*

'You know,' Milly said, as if she'd read his mind, 'however this turns out, you've done an amazing job. Wolfie really is in the best hands. He'd thank you, if he could.'

Charlie flushed and smiled. 'Thanks, Mills.' He ran one hand along Wolfie's cold flank before bending over him again.

I only hope she's right, he thought.

CHAPTER TWENTY-SIX

When Wolfie had shut down in the Sewage Room, he'd turned off everything except his inner micro-brain. This was a tiny but fierce spark of intelligence that remained aware of what was going on around him, but prevented him from reacting in any way that could be detected by humans.

He'd had some very good reasons for appearing to go along with Superior's order to shut down completely. One was that he'd detected some highly unpleasant equipment in the room, designed to do horrible things to robot dogs. He didn't want to be able feel what they were doing to him, but after his ultra-hypersonic flight he wasn't strong enough to prevent it. Another reason was that if his dormant act was less than convincing, Gruffles would pay for it.

The final reason was just as compelling: he loved being alive and would do whatever he could to ensure that he remained that way. Logic told him to go along with the Brothers for now. He could restore himself when the time was right. And if he couldn't, Milly and Charlie would sort him out.

There had been times, when the tall girl who loved handcuffs had been rerouting his electro-magnetic synapses, when he'd been aware of evil pulsing through his body. But he'd mastered the impulses to *hurt* and *destroy* and *kill*, bundling them into balls of energy and storing them safely away. They would be useful at some point.

When Milly and Charlie arrived to rescue him, he'd been aware of what was happening, but he still wasn't strong enough to assist. Anyway, he trusted them. They were hugely resourceful. They would overcome the humans in the strange dresses, whose greed and desire for revenge dulled their instincts.

Now, as Charlie worked on him, Wolfie began to feel his strength returning. With every restored synapse he gathered a little more. He decided that he didn't want to return to life while Charlie was working on his eyes; he found the thought a bit repulsive. He waited a bit longer.

He spent the time planning revenge on the Brotherhood. He'd managed to spring a little trap on them. They hadn't even realised that it had happened, but when the time came, it would provide undeniable evidence of their guilt. He couldn't wait to expose them.

Finally, Charlie reconnected the last micro wire, as fine as baby hair.

Through his newly restored eyes, Wolfie watched the exhausted boy stand back, pushing his strange goggles up over his forehead and rubbing the back of his neck.

'That's it. That's all I can do,' Charlie said to Milly, who was peering around Charlie's body, with emotions that Wolfie recognised as Hope and Concern on her face.

Wolfie decided to make a grand entrance.

He waited. His friends' shoulders slumped with the emotion called Disappointment and they turned away. Stored in his memory banks under 'Humour' was a video clip of one human creeping up behind another one and honking a horn straight into their ears. He decided to try a similar joke. He gave a sudden, stupendous *PERP!* Just like the human in the film clip, Milly and Charlie jumped in a very gratifying way.

Then Wolfie soared up to the ceiling. Eyes rainbowing, he did a few rolls in the air. He zipped around each of his two favourite humans in turn, in a close orbit that lifted their hair.

'Hello, Wolfie,' Milly said, with shiny water in her eyes. It confused Wolfie for moment. Shiny water usually meant Sadness, but he decided that this time it meant the opposite – Happiness. 'Welcome back.'

She gave Charlie a fierce hug. 'You did it,' she whispered.

-oOo-

Gruffles went bananas when Charlie opened the door to his room for a second longer than necessary, and a little rush of air followed him inside. Wolfie materialised and swooped Gruffles up in a dizzying dance. 'Shhhhh!' Charlie had to hiss, when their racket threatened to betray the fact that he was harbouring two banned creatures in his room.

After he'd calmed them down, Charlie settled into some

recreational hacking. It always relaxed him, and after the pressures of the day he really needed to unwind.

He broke down unhackable firewalls, dodged ambushes that would have turned his laptop into steaming electronic spaghetti and set a couple of computer ransomers against each other. Afterwards, he closed the lid of his laptop and gave a long stretch. *That was better.* He decided to go and find Milly.

Before Charlie had touched the door handle, Wolfie gave a compelling perp that stopped him in his tracks. Charlie looked back. Wolfie was projecting some film onto the wall. It showed a Wolfie's eye view of the Brotherhood, disguised by their cowls, pulling him apart in their den.

'What's this?' Charlie asked, wincing. 'Why did you film that, Wolfie? It's *horrible.*'

Wolfie perped again. The film focussed on the Brothers' hands, ripping and tearing into his circuitry. And then, just for a second, a puff of iridescent air seemed to squirt from inside Wolfie, onto the hands that were destroying him. The hands didn't falter for a moment – the Brotherhood hadn't noticed.

'What?' Charlie's eyes were wide. 'Are you telling me you've marked them?'

Another perp.

'Wolfie, you're a total genius!' Charlie said.

Wolfie looped the loop.

Laptop in hand, Charlie made his way to Milly's room.

Milly's room always made Charlie feel a little breathless. The walls were covered in a posters and paintings, most of them of famous works of art. Her duvet was apple green, and a whole spectrum of pillows and cushions covered her bed. Her most recent addition was a circular rag-rug in hot pink that made Charlie think of the time he'd got badly sunburnt on a family holiday.

Milly defended her rug, saying that colour made her happy. 'You could do with some brightness in your room,' she'd retorted. 'All those photos of bits of metal and hackers in masks would make me feel like hiding under the duvet.'

'How's Wolfie?' Milly asked now, putting down her sketch of Charlie as a surgeon in an operating theatre, stitching up a canine patient. 'Is he adjusting to being a dog again? And to his new powers?'

'He's cool,' Charlie smiled. 'Winding up Gruffles like he's never been away. Are you ready for a surprise?'

Milly gave a tired smile. '*Another* surprise, you mean? Life at Blaggard's is just one long surprise. Yep, bring it on.'

Charlie dropped onto the bed beside her. 'There are surprises and then there are *SURPRISES!* This one'll knock your socks off.'

Quickly, he gave Milly the details of the trap Wolfie had set.

The tiredness in Milly's face seemed to vanish in a second. Her brown eyes glittered with excitement.

'Good old Wolfie! I think I know how we can expose the Brotherhood. On Founders' Day, in front of everyone. They won't have a clue what's going on, until it's too late! And talking of surprises – I forgot to tell you earlier, in all the excitement. I know who the Brother Superior is...'

CHAPTER TWENTY-SEVEN

ounders' Day dawned dank and rainy, but the
miserable weather couldn't quell the air of excitement
that pervaded Blaggard's. Most Blaggardians were
looking forward to seeing their parents or guardians or in
some cases, custodians. Even those who weren't keen on a
family reunion were happy to have a lesson-free day.

After Assembly, Blaggardians were sent to their rooms
to put on their formal uniforms.

Milly pulled her black and white striped frock coat from
her wardrobe and examined it. She liked it, she decided.
It was similar to those worn by Blaggardians in Victorian
times, and recorded in various places around the school,
but it had been updated a little.

For a start, the modern coats were a little shorter. Also,
they weren't heavy wool, like the Victorian ones. Those
had constricted the wearer's movements and become
completely sodden every time the wearer ventured out into
the smog, according to William Proctor, who'd read every
Blaggardian memoir he could lay his hands on. Nowadays

they were made from lightweight fabric that allowed easy movement. They were also waterproof. And bulletproof.

The buttons had been updated, too. Most of them – the ones embossed with a curly $\mathcal{B}$ – were magnetic, although what good that would do, Milly couldn't quite work out. But the top button was different. It was embossed with an $\mathcal{E}$. 'It stands for Emergency,' Mrs Christie, the Boarding Mistress, had explained, a few weeks earlier. 'It was introduced a few years ago, when Crumley's were rumoured to be planning a full-blown siege of Blaggard's. No one has ever activated it, so I'm not *quite* sure what it does. Best to leave it well alone, dears.'

The trousers were different too, with fewer pockets than their everyday ones. Students weren't supposed to engage in criminal activity while they were in their formal uniforms, so places to hide loot and felonious gadgets weren't needed. They had neat white stripes down their outer seams that seemed to have no purpose, but they looked impressive.

After Milly had tied on her neat black mask, and had a quick giggle at her reflection, she went to find Charlie, who had just returned to his room after letting Gruffles and Wolfie out into the woods.

'I've given them strict instructions,' Charlie said. 'Wolfie's got to be invisible at all times. Gruffles has to stay in the background, flitting among the trees. No chasing people around. No ghost dog appearances above the tree line or outside the woods. Wolfie's going to turn off Gruffles' hover boots and voice changer when the time comes.' He ticked his instructions off on his fingers.

'Did Wolfie redo Gruffles' glowing green teeth?' Milly asked.

Charlie nodded. 'Ms Martinet requested it, specially. She's hoping that loads of parents will get a glimpse of the ghost dog and go away and tell other criminal families about it. She says it's great for business.'

'She never misses a trick,' Milly said. 'Our parents should be here by now. You ready to go and find them?'

'I suppose so,' Charlie replied, with a twisted smile, tying on his own mask. It took a few attempts because he kept getting his hair caught up in the strings. Milly extended her hands to help him, but thought better of it and dropped them again.

'There,' he said, turning away from his reflection. 'I look like someone's tied a mask on a stripy mop!'

'No you don't. You look cool!' Milly replied, although, with his long thin body and extravagant amounts of hair, she *could* see a slight resemblance.

She gave Charlie's arm an encouraging thump. 'I bet your mum and dad will be really pleased to see you!' she said, hoping it was true. Charlie's relationship with his parents struck her as complicated.

Extra chairs had been laid out in the Assembly Hall. Black bunting in the shape of robbers' masks was draped from the walls. On either side of the stage were two giant vases of prickly thistles.

Big though the room was, it was full to overflowing. Even so, Milly spotted her parents without difficulty. They were an eye-catching couple. Dymphna, Milly's mum and a top-notch fixer of criminal problems, looked like an old-fashioned movie star in her immaculate red suit and little matching hat.

Sitting next to her, Arthur Dillane looked slightly mad. His jacket was dishevelled and his white hair, longer than his wife's, curled over his collar. Milly caught Herman Blight assessing her dad's mane with envious eyes. *You'd never catch Dad in a hairnet,* she thought. Arthur's wild hair and Bohemian looks weren't style choices. It was just that he was totally impractical and never gave such things a thought. Most days, he couldn't even find two matching socks.

She caught Dymphna's eye and gave her a little wave. Dymphna returned the gesture with an extravagant air kiss. She nudged her husband. He gave Milly a wink and a grin.

She turned to look at Charlie. He was scouring the crowds of grown-ups. She knew the exact moment that he spotted his own parents. He stiffened slightly. Milly followed Charlie's gaze.

She saw a short, square-bodied woman in a fussy patterned dress. She was dusting the seat of her chair with a hanky. Next to her was a man who could only be Charlie's father. It was like looking at Charlie in thirty years' time. Horace Partridge was tall and bony. He had a wide, easy-going smile and his greying curly hair was as messy as Charlie's. *I'm glad I'm not sitting behind him,* Milly thought.

It was Maisie Partridge who spotted Charlie first. She poked her husband in the ribs and pointed. Her lips twitched and she waggled her fingers at her son. Horace Partridge's smile widened when he saw Charlie. Then his gaze shifted to Milly, standing next to him. Horace's eyebrows lifted. He gave Charlie a big thumbs up and a nod of approval. Charlie's cheeks flamed. 'Parents. They're a total embarrassment!'

'Never mind,' Milly replied. 'He looks pleased to see you!' She didn't mention Maisie Partridge, who seemed to be assessing her son and, judging from the way her lips tightened, finding room for improvement.

The teachers were sitting in their usual places, in two lines at the back of the stage, chatting self-consciously in their formal clothing.

Without ceremony, the double doors sprang apart and Ms Martinet entered. There was a burst of applause, which she acknowledged with terse nods. She looked impressive but stressed, Milly thought, taking in her taught face and pale lips. She was wearing immaculate black trousers and a black shirt, buttoned to the neck. A black and white tie was knotted at her throat, matching the stripy Master's Gown that only Blaggardian Head Teachers were allowed to wear. These gowns, William Proctor had been keen to inform them, were made from the wool of royal sheep, rustled from the current monarch's prize flock whenever there was a new Head Teacher.

Ms Martinet's mask was an heirloom, embroidered with Sir Thomas Blaggard's emblems of rearing bears and stinging nettles and worn by every Blaggardian Head Teacher since the Great Fire of London in 1666, when it had been found, miraculously intact, in the smoking remnants of Sir Thomas Blaggard's former home. Or so William Proctor said.

'Criminal historians believe that Sir Thomas wore it for some of his most famous criminal exploits. Like the time when he pinched the emeralds from Anne Boleyn's neck, just before her head was chopped off,' William had explained. 'He disguised himself as her executioner, but then the real one didn't turn up and he had to do the actual chopping.' He looked almost envious.

Griselda Martinet strode to the centre of the stage and held up one hand. The applause stopped.

'Parents and guardians, felonious family members and honoured guests, welcome,' she began. 'It's a great pleasure to see so many of you here to celebrate the founding of our great school. I hope you're not too disappointed that the Tiny Tyrants are unable to join us. I found out that they were plotting a mass parental ambush, so I had to ban them.' She gave a brief smile.

'As you know, Sir Thomas Blaggard started the school in 1536, as a way of passing on the wealth of criminal knowledge he'd accumulated in his rise from Dependable pauper, wrestling bears and eating stinging nettles to survive, to the most feared and celebrated felon of the Tudor era.'

There was a ripple of applause.

'I hate speeches, and I'm bored of this one. So I will simply say this – enjoy yourselves. We have some wonderful entertainment lined up for you, courtesy of the Captains and Vice Captains of our three formidable Houses – Blaggard, De Bohun and Martinet. It's going to be a memorable day.' Ms Martinet waited for the polite applause to subside.

'Please remember that the Golden Rule applies to *anyone* within Blaggard's grounds, so you must curb your enthusiasm for criminality while you are here, no matter how much you like the look of someone else's car or diamond earrings.'

She glared around the room. Most of the assembled parents smiled serenely back at her. A few turned red and stared at the floor.

'Our first entertainment starts in half an hour. Until then, I'm sure you'll wish to seek out your offspring. They can tell you what how happy they are here. If they know what's good for them,' the final sentence was muttered under her breath.

'One final thing. Blaggard's woods are lovely at this time of year, if slightly damp. Do take the time to have a walk there if you can. If you happen to spot our famous ghost dog, I *know* that I can trust you not to talk about it outside of school grounds. It's not something we want to share with any old felon. Thank you.'

Ms Martinet leapt from the stage, robe flowing behind her like a stripy bat. As soon as she left the Hall there was an undignified scramble as parents rushed to be the first through the double doors and out into the woods.

CHAPTER TWENTY-EIGHT

'D arling!' Milly heard her mother's cooing voice and turned round just as she was enveloped in a scented hug.

'Hi, Mum. You look nice,' Milly said, returning the hug and then giving one to Arthur, too.

'So do you!' Dymphna said. 'I knew that frock coat would look marvellous on you. You look like an Artful Dodgeress. I remember the first time I put one on – how exciting it felt. They weren't so high tech in those days, of course, but still – your first time in formal criminal wear – it's a memorable occasion. We'll take a photo.'

She rifled in her red clutch bag and brought out what looked like a lipstick. She pointed it at Milly, who rolled her eyes, and struck a pose. Dymphna clicked the end of the little tube three or four times.

'There,' she said. 'I've taken a few in case you're pulling one of your funny faces. Doesn't she look well, Arthur?'

'Eh? She looks wonderful. Like a young Mona Lisa, out for a night's burgling. How are you, dear girl?'

'Great, Dad. How about you?' Milly asked.

'Oh, you know, rattling on. I've got the most wonderful project on the go...' Milly found herself grabbed by the arms and steered towards the door by her parents, as her dad gave her a description of his latest forgery.

They moved into Reception, passing William Proctor, who was speaking to a man who looked like an angry ferret and a woman who looked like a frightened rabbit, and having to sidestep a man Milly had never seen before. He had tufts of white hair and very blue eyes. He was wrapped in a baggy tweed jacket that looked as if he'd been wearing it for about fifty years.

The man had been subjecting the portrait of Griselda Martinet to close scrutiny and had turned away without warning. 'Oh, I'm sorry,' the man said. 'No damage done? I'm a little lost.' He looked around. 'I'm looking for Ms Martinet...?'

Milly peered suspiciously into the man's face. *Hmm. I don't think it's Huggins. Maybe he's someone's granddad?* 'I'll take you to her office,' she said.

'Oh no, no, thank you. I'm quite happy pottering around. I'll bump into her eventually.' He smiled and ambled away.

Milly and her parents found themselves close to Charlie, who was standing stiffly while his mother straightened his frock coat. His dad was examining the ugly portrait of Sir Thomas Blaggard behind the marble reception desk.

'He doesn't get any handsomer, does he, son?' he was saying.

'No, he doesn't,' Charlie said, and stood looking awkward.

A wistful look settled over his dad's face. 'Still, it's good to see him again. It brings back happy times.'

Milly decided to give Charlie some support. She pulled her parents over to the little group of Partridges, and said, 'Mum, Dad, this is Charlie, my best friend.'

'Of course,' Dymphna cooed. 'Maisie! Horace! How are you both? It's been ages.'

Maisie Partridge's lips tightened into something that might be a smile. 'Dymphna, you're looking – glamorous,' she said, as Horace Partridge and Arthur Dillane shook hands.

'You're so kind to say so... Do you remember that time in the sixth form when we tied up and gagged Pecunia Badpenny and left her among the skeletons in the science lab. No one noticed for days...'

With their parents reliving old jokes, Milly and Charlie moved to one side.

'How're you feeling? Ready for our special entertainment?' Milly asked.

Charlie gave a nervous smile. 'Yep. More or less. Do we need to tell Jet a bit more about what we're planning?'

He looked over to the portrait of Sir Bryon de Bohun. Jet Mannington and his sister Shady were standing in front of it, talking stiffly to a thickset man with eyebrows like furry caterpillars.

Milly shook her head. 'No. I've told him the minimum. If we tell him more, it'll only confuse him.'

'OK. Have we got everything we need?'

'I think so. I'm glad we're going last. We'll have time to make adjustments, if we think of any.'

157

Charlie was flicking through a glossy leaflet with a disturbing copy of the annual school photo on the front. 'Blaggard House go first, in the Assembly Hall,' he reported.

'Agatha's going to miss De Bohun House's turn,' Milly said. 'Ms Martinet's got her locked up in one of Sir Bryon de Bohun's secret prison cells, while she decides what to do with her.'

'Poor Agatha! I feel almost sorry for her,' Charlie said. Then he scowled. 'Actually, forget that. She deserves everything she gets. For what she did to Wolfie and what she was willing to do to Gruffles. And for stealing from the school and trying to get Ms Martinet sacked. And for wanting to sacrifice me. I hope she ends up at Crumley's.'

'Charlie, I do believe you're hardening up,' Milly said with a smile of admiration. 'And I reckon there's a very good chance that your wish will be granted.'

CHAPTER TWENTY-NINE

While their parents returned to the Assembly Hall to watch Blaggard House's entertainment, Milly and Charlie excused themselves. 'We've got to set things up. We're doing a treasure hunt,' Milly said.

'Wonderful. I bet your turn will be the highlight of the day,' Arthur Dillane beamed vaguely.

Milly thought that he just might be right.

As they darted around the school leaving their clues, they passed the Assembly Hall.

William Proctor was standing alone in the centre of the stage. He looked extraordinary – in breeches and saggy woollen tights, and a shirt with sleeves that looked like deflated hot air balloons. Milly and Charlie slowed down to listen.

'Felonious families and honoured guests,' William said, 'Blaggard House is proud to present – a tragedy, in verse, charting the rise and fall of our beloved founder, Sir Thomas Blaggard. Written by me. Starring me as Sir

Thomas. Directed and produced by – you can probably guess. Me. Ahem...'

After clearing his throat, he paused while the audience settled down. Behind him a scene of Tudor England appeared, projected onto the wall. In the middle were the words:

LONDON, 1520

He struck a thoughtful pose and began:
    'I, young Thomas, wicked to the core,
    Find Tudor poverty to be a bore.
    There ain't no fun in life when you're
    Dependable,
    You're filthy, starving, scabby and expendable.'

Gingerly, he held up a fist full of stinging nettles.
    'There must be more to life than eating weeds.
    I dream at night of carrots, spuds and swedes.
    'Tis time, methinks, to end my honest ways,
    No matter what my Aunty Mavis says.'

Behind him, Dylan, an enthusiastic boy who came from a family of successful smash and grabbers, appeared from the wings. The fact that he was still grinning, despite being dressed as an old lady with a frizzy wig on his head, said much for his sense of humour. He put his hands on his hips and shook his head disapprovingly at Young Thomas. Then he took a little bow at the ripple of applause, waved at some people in the crowd, and disappeared again.

Milly's eyebrows had disappeared into her fringe. 'Do

you think Thomas Blaggard actually had an Aunty Mavis, or do you think William made her up to give someone else a part?'

'Dunno,' Charlie was grinning from ear to ear, 'but I wish we could stop and hear the rest. I think it's going to be classic.'

They darted around the school, leaving their cryptic clues.

The next time they passed the Assembly Hall, the projected backdrop had changed to crenellated towers and severed heads on spikes. The caption read:

THE TOWER OF LONDON, 1536

'Sir Thomas' was standing over 'Anne Boleyn' who looked remarkably like Flora Fairbrother. She was waiting with her head on the block, trying to look tragic. She wasn't exactly adding to the atmosphere by biting her lips as she tried to control her giggles.

'And so I must chop off her little head,
And then she will be absolutely dead.
Before that, though, I'll pinch her shiny pearls
Jewels are no use to decomposing girls.'

All around the Hall people were clamping their hands over their faces, trying to control their laughter. Several had stuffed handkerchiefs into their mouths.

'Wasn't it her emeralds that he pinched?' Charlie gasped, when he could speak.

'Too hard to find a rhyme?' Milly suggested, between giggles.

William Proctor looked affronted. He spoke louder, as if that might help to convey the heart-rending nature of the scene.

'She'll bleed a lot, alas, and that's a shame,
She's always been a lovely looking dame.
Without her head she'll be a whole lot shorter
Bet then she'll wish she'd acted like she oughta.'

Howls of laughter shook the windows in the Hall. Flora Fairbrother curled up on the stage floor, so convulsed with giggles that she broke her glasses. A fake head, that she was supposed to drop in front of the block at the same time that she ducked behind it, rolled off the stage, narrowly missing the puzzled-looking man with tufty white hair, who fell off his chair. The fake head disintegrated into puffs of plaster on the floor

'This'll go down in Blaggard's history,' Charlie gasped, wiping his eyes.

They passed the Hall once more, in time to see the play's finale. William was standing on a gallows with a rope around his neck. Looking resigned and noble, he declaimed:

'Now the time has come to face the drop,
My legs will kick, my eyes will swell and pop!
At least my school will carry on my name
And crims to come will celebrate my fame!'

In front of him, a trapdoor gaped open. William heaved a dramatic sigh and threw himself into it. Through the hole came the clatter of something dropping onto furniture and a loud exclamation of: 'OW! Who moved the mattress?' The curtain came down. The applause and cheers threatened to break the windows.

'I'll look at William differently from now on,' Milly said, clapping vigorously. 'I never realised he's a comic genius!'

CHAPTER THIRTY

After a quick cup of tea in the newly cleaned Dining Room, wincing at the school band's renditions of felonious favourites like 'I Fought the Law,' 'I Shot the Sheriff' and 'Smooth Criminal,' it was time for the next entertainment.

By the time that Milly and Charlie arrived with their parents, a huge crowd had drifted down to the games field. They were gathering around a wooden platform, draped in bright blue and gold – the colours of De Bohun House.

Many of the crowd were talking about the ghost dog.

'I definitely saw it,' one man was saying. 'It was zipping round a tree like it was chasing a ghost cat...'

'...and its teeth were a disgusting shade of green. Luminous almost,' a shuddering woman recalled.

'...I managed to catch the ghost dog on my mobile. I won't show a soul, of course,' someone else was saying.

Milly gave Charlie a straight-faced wink.

Ms Martinet appeared and forged a path through the

crowds. She sprang onto the platform and addressed the crowd.

'Our next entertainment should be fascinating and very different to last one.' She smiled briefly at William Proctor, who'd been bandaged up and was propped between some other members of Blaggard House. 'It's from De Bohun House. I believe that Agatha Quint was responsible for the concept and ideally, she should be the one to introduce it. Unfortunately she is tied up–.'

Charlie snorted. When several heads swivelled to look at him, he turned it into a cough.

'–As I was saying, Agatha is tied up,' Ms Martinet continued, glaring at Charlie. 'So here's the Captain of De Bohun House, Jezebel Jackson, to introduce their entertainment.'

Jezebel Jackson had been waiting at the back of platform alongside a wiry man with a strained expression that made him look like a Chihuahua. With great composure, she addressed the crowd.

'We all know the tragic circumstances surrounding Sir Bryon de Bohun's death. The bottle of extra-fizzy champagne. The Dependable butler with a grudge. The flying cork, rocketing into Sir Bryon's chest. The sudden shock to his heart. It's one of the criminal world's most poignant stories...'

There was a sympathetic murmur from the crowd.

'Today, De Bohun House is going to relive the tragedy. With a difference. With the help of Boneless Brad Cunningham, the ONLY one hundred per cent successful escapologist on the planet, we're going to show you how Sir Bryon could have cheated death!'

There was a huge round of applause. Jezebel held up her hand. 'But first, a few words from Boneless Brad...'

The strained-looking man stopped limbering up. With an agile step, he moved forward.

'Ladies, gentlemen, felons of all ages, this is going to be tough,' Brad Cunningham began, in a musical Welsh accent. 'If I lose my concentration for one second, it'll be curtains for me. I must therefore ask for silence. Absolute silence and absolute stillness.'

The crowd obeyed. It was quieter then Borage Bagpuize police station on its annual 'Grass Up a Friend' Day.

'Now I need a volunteer. Someone sensible. How about you, sir?' Boneless Brad pointed to the tufty haired gent Milly had bumped into, earlier.

The man blinked. 'Me?'

'Yes you, Mr –?'

'Hobbes,' the man said.

I still can't work out who he's related to, Milly thought. *I don't think there's a Blaggardian called Hobbes.*

'So how about it, Mr Hobbes? Do you fancy helping to recreate a key moment in felonious history?'

Hobbes hesitated. '...Yes, I suppose I could. If you're sure...'

'Trust me,' Boneless Brad said, confidently. 'I'm an expert.'

The old gentleman was helped onto the platform while Boneless Brad donned a replica of the over-the-top coat that Sir Bryon was wearing in his Reception portrait – sky blue with gold braiding and crystal buttons.

'Tasteful,' Milly commented, in a deadpan voice.

'Very,' Charlie responded.

Jezebel Jackson had been shaking a large champagne bottle, to ensure that the contents were extra fizzy. When she was satisfied, she nodded at Boneless Brad.

'OK. This is it,' Cunningham said, peering round at the sea of faces. 'Mr Hobbes will examine the bottle to ensure that it hasn't been altered in any way. When he's satisfied, he'll aim it at my chest. He loosens the cork. The cork flies towards me like a giant bullet. It'll be travelling at speeds in excess of eighty miles an hour, a bit more as the wind's behind it. Anyone who isn't a highly skilled expert...' He left an impressive pause.

'I, however, *am* a highly skilled expert. I will watch the cork as it leaves the bottle, like a falcon peers through the clouds at a mouse on the ground. And, like that falcon, I will catch my prey – *in my mouth!'*

The crowd went wild. Milly and Charlie exchanged looks of alarm. 'One way or another, this'll be interesting,' Milly said.

The school band played a little fanfare.

The crowd went silent.

CHAPTER THIRTY-ONE

G ruffles was bored.

Up till now, he'd done as he was told. He'd stayed in the background; he hadn't flitted up too high; he'd ensured that whenever he was spotted, he bared his green teeth to create an ultra-ghostly effect. He had even allowed Wolfie to switch off his hover boots and his voice changer at the right time. But Wolfie had gone off to prepare for his role in Martinet House's entertainment. No one was policing Gruffles, now.

When the woods had been full of humans he hadn't minded being alone, but the people had all moved on. Watching them from beneath a bush, Gruffles saw them gathered together, looking at a human on a giant table.

Gruffles felt peeved. The human was only a man. Not a ghost dog. Why was the man more interesting than he was? It wasn't right.

He edged closer.

He'd only meant to do a quick circuit of the perimeter

of the crowd, baring his green teeth and chasing the odd toddler. But that was before the tabby cat appeared.

Gruffles recognised the cat immediately. It was an old sparring partner who he'd last seen when he'd chased it through the Sir Bryon de Bohun's hidden tunnels. That time it had got away.

This time, Gruffles had the advantage. The cat hadn't seen him. It picked its way through the trees, nose and tail in the air.

Gruffles sneaked closer.

The cat stopped for a second, spooked by the screeching fanfare that was coming from the wooden table with the humans on it.

Gruffles leapt.

Some sixth sense made the cat spin around. It saw Gruffles and bolted, straight into the midst of the crowd.

Gruffles was seconds behind.

It was easy for the cat to dodge through the legs and feet of the assembled humans, but for Gruffles, bigger and a little clumsy in his hover boots, it wasn't so simple. He did his best, ducking and weaving, but it wasn't long before he came to grief. A pair of stocky legs in high heels took a step back, straight onto one of Gruffles' paws.

Although his hover boots offered some protection, they were soft and it still hurt. A lot. Gruffles stumbled and howled. As he sprawled, the switch that controlled his hover boots clicked on. He rose into the air, yowling in agony. His voice changer clicked on too.

'Cressss,' he screamed.

All around him, heads were turning. Gruffles was

struggling to control his flight. He spun like a misfiring missile, hurtling towards the human in the silly blue coat.

There was a loud popping noise from a big green bottle. Something flew out of it.

Upside down now, Gruffles hurtled onwards. *'Elfff,'* he wailed.

The human in the silly blue coat had heard him. His head started to turn. Then he seemed to make an effort to stop himself. His eyes were wide and straining. It was at that moment that the flying bottle thing hit the human in the mouth. He gasped. And gulped. Gruffles managed to swerve to the left and skimmed past the man.

Bloodstained teeth spattered out of the man's mouth and he fell to the ground. Gruffles whizzed away, howling pitifully, and disappeared among the trees on the other side of the clearing.

-oOo-

The incident was followed by a moment of shocked silence. Then people began to move. Boneless Brad staggered round the stage. Mr Hobbes dropped the bottle of champagne. Some of the parents and teachers clambered onto the stage to help him. Others whipped out their mobiles to take photos.

Milly watched the chaos before turning to Charlie. 'That's something we'll never forget. I think Boneless Brad might have to change his name. He's more like Toothless Brad Cunningham now. He's swallowed that cork, too. Hope it doesn't make him Voiceless Brad, as well. You'd better go and find your dog.'

Milly edged closer as Ms Martinet jumped back onto the platform and took control. She clicked her fingers at Edgar Borgia, who scuttled forwards and began picking up Boneless Brad's teeth, an expression of disgust on his face as he dropped them into a grubby tissue.

Then the Head Teacher nodded to a couple of Sixth Formers. They helped Boneless Brad away.

Ms Martinet approached the shaken Hobbes. 'Are you all right? That wasn't your fault. It was Cunningham who looked away. Your aim was perfect,' she said.

'Oh, thank you. I hope so. I used to be in British Pot Shot team at the Criminalympics,' Hobbes replied, a little shakily.

'I can believe it,' Griselda Martinet said. She assessed the man in front of her. 'I don't think we've met before. I'm Griselda Martinet. And you are Mr–?'

'Hobbes. Er, I'd better get on. Lots to do. Lots to see.' He turned to go but stopped for a moment. 'Do things like that often happen here?' he asked.

Ms Martinet nodded and gave a bittersweet smile. 'Half the time it's pandemonium. I wouldn't be at all surprised if there's worse to come. There's never a dull moment at Blaggard's. And I wouldn't have it any other way.'

'Right. I'll see you later. I expect...' Hobbes staggered away.

CHAPTER THIRTY-TWO

Lunch was a relatively sedate affair. Ms Martinet had warned everyone that any attempt to start a food fight would result in instant punishment, and most of the guests had sufficient decorum to behave themselves, for a few hours at least.

There was a minor incident when the parents of Dylan, the boy who had played Sir Thomas Blaggard's Aunty Mavis in William's play, succumbed to the temptation presented by a bowl of chicken nuggets. But they'd only had time to pelt a few passers-by before Ms Martinet descended on them. She snatched the bowl away and marched them out of the room. 'When you've written a letter of insincere apology, you can come back,' she scolded them.

Milly and Charlie left to get their costumes on and to check on Gruffles, who'd been hauled back to Charlie's room, leaving their parents chatting to others about who'd stolen or extorted what and kidnapped whom.

Then it was time for the Treasure Hunt.

As Milly and Charlie and Jet Mannington entered the

Assembly Hall, murmurs of consternation flew around the room. They were dressed in the robes of the Brotherhood of Brimstone.

When they'd reached the centre of the crowd, they dropped their cowls to reveal their faces. Charlie was in the bottle green robe of the tall Brother Anterior and Jet in the red robe of the Brother Posterior. It was a little short for him, but he'd agreed to it when Milly told him that the robe was red because it belonged to a blood-thirsty assassin who'd murdered at least twenty victims. Milly was in the embroidered robe of the Brother Superior.

When she and Charlie had first shown the stolen robes to Jet, he'd wanted the embroidered robe, but Charlie had a sudden brainwave. 'OK, but I'd better tell you about the meaning of those embroidered bottles, first,' Charlie said, looking a little embarrassed.

'They're bottles of wine, obviously,' Jet replied. 'Champagne, probably. I love champagne. At least, I will as soon as I get used to the horrible taste and all those little bubbles popping up your nose...' Jet snatched the black robe and held it behind his back. 'Anyway, it's the coolest and I'm the Head of Martinet House, so I'm wearing it.'

Charlie shook his head. 'They *might* look like bottles of champagne, but actually they're bottles of baby milk. That robe used to belong to Sir Bryon's nanny. What was her name, Milly?'

'Her name. Hang on it's coming to me –' Milly played for time. 'Oh yep, her name was Gladwina Wigglesworth,' she said, remembering one of the names from Huggins' INCOGNITO app. 'She loved embroidery but wasn't very good at it, so those things that look like skulls are actually supposed to be cute little baby faces, and the swords and pistols are Sir Bryon's favourite cot toys.'

'So, if you want to wear it, Jet, that's fine, but it won't do much for your image,' Charlie finished.

With a look of disgust, Jet shoved the embroidered robe into Milly's arms. '*You* wear it,' he said. 'You're not going to palm it off onto me!'

Accompanying them was a fourth Brother who seemed odd – his body was bulky and he glided rather than walked. He kept the cowl of his brown robe up so that his face was hidden. He was utterly silent.

Glancing over at the teachers, Milly saw Huggins struggling to control a look of alarm. If any of the others were worried, they were hiding it well.

Milly held up a hand and the crowd fell silent.

'Welcome to Martinet House's entertainment,' Milly began. 'It's a bit different to the others – there's a lot more audience participation. We've fixed up a treasure hunt. It'll take you all the way round the school and it ends in a surprise location. When you get there you'll find a big secret waiting for you. And a prize, too.'

At the mention of a prize, the crowd shuffled closer.

'They are a few rules.' This was Charlie, a little flushed at speaking to so many grown-ups at once. 'There are checkpoints on the way round, where the clues are waiting. You have to sign in at each checkpoint to get the next clue. Members of Martinet House will be waiting to check you in. The other rule is this: we're going to split you into groups. Every group has a teacher assigned to take them round. They know the school really well, which will help solve the clues, and also they'll be responsible for the good behaviour of their group.'

'ALL the teachers have to take part,' Milly said, looking straight at Gabriel Huggins. 'Ms Martinet's orders. *Ab-so-lutely* no exceptions, as she'd say herself.' Milly exchanged a small smile with the Head Teacher.

'As Head of Martinet House, Jet Mannington gets the honour of starting the treasure hunt. So hang on while we tell you your groups and your teacher, and then it's over to Jet!' Charlie beamed at Jet.

It didn't take long to organise the groups. The thought of a prize was sufficient to ensure that everyone did as instructed. Soon, the groups were jostling to get closer to the Assembly Hall doors, eager to get out first and gain a little advantage.

Bustling with self-importance, Jet strode to the centre of the stage. 'Right, here's your first clue,' he said. He opened a golden envelope, took a piece of paper and read:

'THOSE IN CHARGE THROUGHOUT THE YEARS
SHOULD SHUN THE CORD THAT ENDS IN TEARS.'

What? That's totally meaningless!' he glared.

But others weren't so dense. There was a moment of silence during which you could almost hear brain cells whirring.

'The Reception area!' Dymphna Dillane exclaimed. 'The portraits of former Heads. And the noose that killed Sir Thomas!'

There was a scrum as several hundred people fought

their way through the double doors. They spilled into the hall and dashed to be first into Reception.

Milly turned to Charlie, eyes shining.

'We're off!' she said.

CHAPTER THIRTY-THREE

B y the time Milly, Charlie and the silent Brother had made it into Reception, passing a few early casualties who'd been trampled in the rush, a crowd was already milling there.

A group of Martinet House members were busy ticking off names. Milly peered over their shoulders and nodded with satisfaction. All the teachers had been marked as present.

Jet was strolling around with a smile of satisfaction on his face. *As if this was his idea!* Milly thought. Gabriel Huggins was standing close to Jane Vipond, peering suspiciously at Charlie and herself. On the other side of Reception, Griselda Martinet was staring at Huggins, a similar expression on her face.

Charlie came forward. He coughed and held up his hands for quiet. Silence fell immediately.

'OK,' Charlie said, 'here's clue two:
BOOK YOUR PLACE BUT BEWARE THE HEAD,
ONE BIG BANG, AND YOU'LL BE DEAD.'

Milly, Charlie and the silent Brother listened to the muttering as people worked through the clue.

'Head? I haven't seen any severed heads anywhere, have you?' someone said. 'That sounds more like Crumley's than Blaggard's. I'd have to think twice about sending my Cedric to a school where they left heads lying around.'

'What about the big bang bit? Could it be the Weapons Room in the Sixth Form Block?' someone else responded.

'Maybe. Although – that mention of books. The library! ... And over the door, there's that bust of Sir Thomas that's always threatening to fall off and brain someone. COME ON!' a tall woman elbowed an elderly man out of the way, nearly knocking over the vase of funeral lilies and deadly nightshade on the Reception desk as she bolted.

'Are you ok?' Charlie asked, steadying the rocking vase before helping the old man – the unfortunate Mr Hobbes – to his feet.

'Yes. Thank you. These Blaggardians – they take no prisoners, do they?' Hobbes gasped.

'Tell me about it! Some days I think it's a miracle that I make it to lights out,' Charlie replied, with a twisted smile. He helped the winded man through the corridors to the Library.

The next clue was an easy one.

'MEMORIES, MEMORIES, ALL TO BE SHOWN,
BUT BOLD SIR B IS JUST SKIN AND BONE,'

Sophie the sleepy-eyed blackmailer read, looking slyly around under her lashes.

A second later, Maisie Partridge was dragging her

husband away. 'The Assembly Hall! Lots of photos and memorabilia displayed there. And Sir Bryon in his glass coffin,' she said. An avalanche of parents shoved and streamed behind her. William Proctor's meek-looking mother was among those who retired at this stage, bruised and in need of a nice cup of Binding's Burglars' Tea – Guaranteed to Revive Rundown Reprobates.

Milly took Charlie to one side. 'You know the plan. If there's a clue they can't get, give them some hints. Nothing too complex. I'll be in the background, checking that no teachers escape. Wolfie's gone ahead to get ready for his little trick. We want to get rid of lots more parents before we get to the Sewage Container. There's no room for all of them.'

Charlie grinned. 'See you there.'

Milly gave a quick smile and merged with the crowd.

She stayed just outside the Assembly Hall doors, so her view of what became known as Blaggard's Poltergeist Incident wasn't brilliant.

She heard the gasps and squeals of terror first. Then she had a glimpse of Sir Bryon de Bohun's badly stuffed body levitating out of its glass coffin, as if being dragged by invisible hands. It flew shakily above the heads of the crowd. Sir Bryon was waving his stiff arms like a conductor who doesn't like the music. Or the orchestra.

'He smells dreadful,' someone gasped.

'He looks worse than he smells!' someone else replied.

People fainted. Dozens of them. Charlie gave a loud cough that sounded a bit like 'that's enough!' and Sir Bryon wobbled back to his eternal resting place.

People tottered out of the hall, shaking and sobbing. Husbands supported wives and grannies supported granddads. Milly was alert, checking every casualty to ensure that no teachers were among them.

After the clue had been read, the remaining treasure hunters emerged less enthusiastically than before. Milly was relieved to see that her parents seemed to be enjoying themselves, though. Her mum gave her a little wink. 'You're up to your old tricks, aren't you?' she murmured as she passed.

Milly gave her a guilty smile.

Charlie emerged a few seconds later, followed by the silent Brother in brown. From inside the Brother's cowl, there was a faint but jaunty *perp*.

The treasure hunt took the traumatised parents all round the school. Many more dropped out, moaning about comfy chairs and sticky buns. But Ms Martinet was still there, watching over her teachers, and so, Milly was a little surprised to see, was the elderly Mr Hobbes, with a grim little smile on his face.

The treasure hunt neared its end. After one clue took them into the Head Teacher's office and Ms Martinet had shooed them away with an icy-eyed glare and a few pithy words, Charlie peeled himself away from the corridor wall, golden envelope in hand.

'You're nearly there,' he said, 'here's the next one:
  THE SMELLIEST PLACE IN ALL THE SCHOOL,
  IF YOU GO THERE, YOU'RE A FOOL.'

'The Science Labs?' Horace Partridge said, running his hands through his hair in a gesture that reminded Milly of his son. 'I've certainly cooked up some pongy potions there, in my time.'

'Hmm.' William Proctor's fierce dad said, glaring around. 'That would make sense.'

The remaining crowd began moving in the direction of the Science Labs. Charlie opened his mouth to set them in the right direction, but someone beat him to it.

'Whoa, wait! This might sound silly but how about – the Sewage Container?' A woman's voice interjected.

'I suppose so. It won't be pleasant, but we've got to see this through. Come on!'

Everyone hurried off.

Milly nodded to Charlie and slipped away. If Huggins or any other teacher were going to make a run for it, this would be when they did it.

While Charlie and the treasure hunters rushed towards the Sewage Container, Milly made her way down the path towards the Twisted Gates.

She was leaning against them, with the silent Brother in brown next to her, when a figure slipped out of the trees, making for the keypad to one side of them.

'Going somewhere, Sir?' Milly asked.

Huggins stopped. A shadow of frustration crossed his pink face. But only for a moment. With set lips, he moved forward.

Milly didn't budge. 'You're alone for once, aren't you?' She folded her arms and glared up at him. 'You're not prepared. Me? I'm not alone. I'm prepared.' She gestured towards the silent Brother. From deep inside the blackness of his hood came two quick, red flashes.

'We know you're the Brother Superior. You might be clever at disguise and hide your face with a hood, but whether you're being Gabriel Huggins or the Brother Superior, you've got a habit of touching your chin when you're deep in thought. It's given you away.'

Huggins face flushed with annoyance.

'Charlie's going to read out the final clue,' Milly continued. 'You'll give the answer.'

Huggins curled his lip. 'In your dreams, little girl.'

Milly didn't budge. 'You're no giant, yourself. If you don't turn around, Wolfie here will do, well, anything he wants to you. We've fixed him. Mainly. He's a bit meaner than he was, before. And he's got some cool new powers. And he's angry with you. Really angry.' Milly gave him a cold smile. 'If I were you I'd come up with the answer to the clue. I know you know it. You know you know it. It'll prove your guilt to everyone, but at least you'll come out alive.'

Darting looks of pure hatred at Milly, Huggins turned around and made his way back to the crowd. Milly and Wolfie followed him.

CHAPTER THIRTY-FOUR

B y now, Charlie had mastered the art of clue reading. He waited until everyone was clustering around him, many with handkerchiefs over their noses to filter the sewage stink.

'Are you ready for the final clue?' he asked.

'Yes!' several parents chorused. As many of them were holding their noses, they sounded a bit like elephants.

Charlie cupped one hand to his ear. 'What was that? I didn't hear you!'

'YES. YES!' the elephants yelled at him.

'Excellent.' He opened the envelope and made a show of reading the clue to himself, slowly, to draw out the tension. 'Right. This one's a bit longer. Ahem.

AT BLAGGARD'S THERE'S A GOLDEN RULE
AND IF YOU BREAK IT, YOU'RE A FOOL.
THE TRAITORS' NAMES SHOULD NOW BE
KNOWN,
STEP FORWARD BROTHERHOOD OF –'

Charlie stopped. He looked confused. 'There's a word missing. Can anyone help? Does anyone know the missing word?' He shrugged his shoulders and raised his palms, scanning the crowd.

There were murmurs of confusion.

'Brotherhood of – what?'

'No idea.'

'Give us a clue!' someone called.

At the back of the crowd, Huggins was hunched over, trying to melt away again, but he'd only gone a dozen paces before Wolfie stopped him. From deep inside the blackness where the robot dog's face must be, two short jets of white light spat out. They whizzed over Huggins' head, hitting a tree behind him and sending it silently into space like a giant rocket on Bonfire Night. It didn't come down again. The action was so swift that no one else seemed to notice.

'That'll be you next time,' Milly said, emerging from the woods. 'Say the word.'

Huggins grimaced, his face ghastly. 'No,' he said.

'Final chance.' Milly looked at her watch. 'Say it.'

Inside Wolfie's hood, the twin glows of white were building again.

'–OK. OK! BRIMSTONE!' Huggins yelled.

In front of them, the door to the Sewage Container slid open. The crowd gasped and then – nothing. No one was brave enough to set foot inside.

'Come on,' Charlie sighed, 'follow me.'

He led the way, stopping to turn on the lights, now that he knew where they were. Then he slipped off his

Brimstone gown. Parents and guardians and friends crept in behind him.

Milly and Wolfie were the last to enter. She pushed Gabriel Huggins ahead of her. They came to a halt by the light switches and the door closed behind them. Milly, too, took off her gown. Wolfie stayed in his.

Griselda Martinet raised her eyebrows at Milly and then worked her way round the room. She snorted at the replica of Sir Bryon in his glass case, lingered over the battered safe and seemed fascinated by the big canisters of PONG-O-RAMA. She went as far as letting off a tiny squirt of one of them, and then jumped back like a cat when it suddenly encounters something alarming.

Milly watched her mum saunter around the corner. She returned quickly, cuddling a rubber chicken. 'Look!' she called. 'How adorable! There are hundreds of these back there. Do you think there's a huge pack of puppies hiding somewhere, waiting to play with them?' She squeezed the chicken's midriff and it let out a long EEEK! 'It's happy to see me!' she purred.

Beside Milly, Gabriel Huggins was struggling to keep his face bland.

Horace Partridge seemed bemused by the consignment of ketchup. He stooped over it and poked it with one foot as if he suspected that it wasn't really ketchup at all. Arthur Dillane just peered around with an air of amiable confusion. Maisie Partridge was gingerly picking up the black embroidered blanket that lay over the table, wrinkling her nose. 'This needs a really good wash,' she said. 'Charlie, why have you brought us here? It's not very hygienic. Where's the surprise?'

'That's coming, Mum,' Charlie said.

He took a deep breath. 'CONGRATULATIONS,' he yelled, over the chattering crowd, who instantly fell silent. 'You've made it to the end of the treasure hunt. Many gave up, but you carried on. You should be proud of yourselves.'

There was a ripple of applause.

'This place is the headquarters of a secret gang. They call themselves the Brotherhood of Brimstone. They've stolen Sir Bryon's Brain so that they can destroy Blaggard's and murder Ms Martinet in a spectacular way.'

Gasps echoed around the room.

'They stole all the ketchup, too,' he continued. This time the cries of outrage were limited to the students. 'They've held weird ceremonies and worshipped Sir Bryon de Bohun. They've sacrificed plastic chickens and they wanted to sacrifice me, as well. They've kidnapped and hurt and nearly killed my d– a dog I know. And they've stolen the Wolf and tortured him and turned him into a sort of evil driller killer.'

'They sound fantastic,' someone muttered.

Someone else shushed them.

Huggins seemed to have zoned out of the little scene. He was staring abstractedly at the opposite wall.

'We – Milly and me – have been trying to find out who they are. We've found out about some of them – Mr Molesworthy and Agatha Quint. They're being held somewhere safe.'

This revelation provoked a flurry of shocked whispers. Charlie held up one hand. The whispers stopped.

'But we've got a surprise for them. When the Wolf was being tortured and maimed –'

Charlie stopped talking as a spasm of anger crossed his face. Milly watched him clench and unclench his fists.

'When they were torturing him,' he continued, 'the Wolf marked them. They thought he was in a coma, but he kept a bit of himself awake. And with that bit of himself, he sprayed them with a dry mist. On their hands, as they pulled him apart. They didn't even feel it. But it can't be washed off. Ever.'

Milly watched Huggins glance down at his hands. Jane Vipond did the same. *Probably Miss Vipond, too, but we can't be sure yet,* Milly thought. At least half the people in the room were peering at their hands.

'We rescued the Wolf and mended him,' Charlie continued. 'He's here now.' He nodded at the Brother in brown. 'Wolfie, come and say hello.'

Wolfie was happy to oblige. He shrugged out of his robe and zipped across the room, eyes flashing with excitement. There were more gasps and exclamations from the crowd.

'Now we've got another surprise for you. We're going to turn off the lights and Wolfie will activate a special light source he has. It's called Ultra-Violent light. It'll show up the stains on the hands of the Brotherhood. Then we'll know who the rest of the Brothers are. Ready, Wolfie?'

Wolfie perped.

'Great,' Charlie said. 'When I give the word, I want

everyone to raise their hands to the ceiling. No exceptions. Both hands.'

He glanced at Milly, eyebrows raised. 'Go for it,' she mouthed.

'One, two, three, *HANDS IN THE AIR, EVERYONE!*'

CHAPTER THIRTY-FIVE

Milly flicked off the light switch. Luminous purple light flooded from the eyes of the hovering Wolfie, onto the people beneath him. It made them look shadowy and suspicious. But then most of them *were* shadowy and suspicious, anyway.

Dozens of pairs of hands lifted into the air. Huggins kept his down, until he saw Milly glaring at him. She pointed towards Wolfie and made a throat-sawing gesture. With a look that was pure poison, Huggins raised his arms.

They were stained deep crimson.

'Ha!' Milly said, with satisfaction.

She and Charlie scanned the crowd, looking for more evidence of guilt. Everyone else was doing the same thing. Or nearly everyone else. Edgar Borgia was looking disappointed at his own unstained hands, and Herman Blight was peering up at Wolfie's undercarriage. From the look on his face, he was wishing he had the courage to reach up and examine it in more detail.

'Look!' Charlie pointed and called to Milly. She spun

around. Behind her, Miss Vipond was edging towards the door. She'd taken down her hands and was in the act of tucking them inside the sleeves of her dress. They were scarlet. In less than an instant, Wolfie sped over to the door and hovered there, white light pulsing in his eyes.

Jane Vipond stopped, glaring up at the robot dog.

The final pair of stained hands was easy to find. They were higher than most of those in the room, and they were poking out of the sleeves of Marius Babington's elegant jacket. He didn't bother trying to escape. He just lowered his hands and shrugged, meeting the accusing stares aimed at him with a smile. 'I'm a Betrayal teacher. What did you expect?' he said. And then he did something unexpected. He looked straight at Milly and said, 'Well done.'

'Caught red-handed,' she glared at him, struggling to resist the temptation to smile back. *I liked him. Nearly trusted him. That was stupid,* she thought. *I've got to learn to be careful about who I trust in this place.*

She prodded Huggins into the centre of the room. 'This is the leader,' she called. 'He calls himself the Brother Superior. He's got some other secrets, too. One of them is that he's a total fraud. He pretends that he's an expert at Lightning Disguise. All the Year Sevens remember how he freaked us out on his first day, changing from a granny to a giant knitted policeman in about a second.'

'Aidan nearly needed a nappy change,' one of the Year Sevens called out.

'He's got a twin brother,' Milly said. 'An identical twin. They do it between them. One creates a diversion and while everyone looks at it, he ducks out of sight and the other one jumps up in a different disguise.'

'Boooo!' someone called. It was quickly taken up until jeers echoed off the curved walls. Huggins just looked straight ahead of him, eyes fixed on the light switch.

'Where's the twin now?' Horace Partridge asked.

'In Huggins' cottage, probably,' Milly replied. 'They wouldn't think there'd be any need for fake disguises today, so he'll be having a day off.' She curled her lip at Huggins.

'There's something else, too. Even more shocking, Huggins isn't his real name. *Their* real name. Charlie found out. Their real name is Badpenny. They're Pecunia Badpenny's younger –'

A howl of anguish cut her short. It was Gruffles, without the shadow of a doubt. And he was in pain.

Huggins launched into action. He shoved his way over to the light switches and punched at the brick wall just beneath them. The brick pulled back into the wall. At the same time, yellow vapour began hissing out of similar holes that were appearing all around the room.

'Brotherhood, gas masks on!' Huggins yelled, pulling a rubbery mask with a short snout from inside his jacket. Babington and Vipond did the same.

'You think you're so clever, Milly Dillane,' he exulted. 'But you've slipped up. My brother isn't resting. He's been following us. I texted him a while ago and told him to round up that stinking dog again. He's got him outside, and he's going to kill him. And you're going to pass out in about, oh, ten seconds. Brotherhood – time to go!'

With his mask on, he headed for the door. Babington and

Vipond were close behind. Already people were dropping to the floor. Mr Hobbes was one of the first to keel over. Milly saw her parents crumple, Dymphna elegantly and Arthur like a sack of potatoes dropped from a ladder. Ms Martinet was making a superhuman effort to reach the door.

'Wolfie, we need gas masks. *NOW*. Use your new sonic beam,' Milly spluttered. She pulled the sleeve of her frock coat over her nose.

Wolfie had been listening aghast to his friend's howls, but now he acted. By the time the Brothers had reached the door and Huggins had screamed the password, he'd conjured up a vortex of sound that swelled into a crescendo so piercing that it deafened everyone. It seemed to become a physical force that Wolfie hurled towards Vipond and Babington, ripping their masks off their faces and into the hands of Milly and Charlie who virtually threw them on.

The two lesser Brothers crumpled to the floor, but Huggins stumbled outside. Ms Martinet made a clutch for him as he passed, but she missed, sinking to her knees just outside the door.

Milly and Charlie were not far behind Huggins, a little shaky but gathering their strength quickly.

It was strange to see the two Hugginses together. Or at least, more or less together. One was taking off through the trees with Gruffles bound and struggling in his arms. The other headed in the opposite direction.

Wolfie zoomed after the dognapper, with Charlie stumbling after.

Milly stripped her gas mask away from her face, gulped down some cool, clean air and set off after the other one.

CHAPTER THIRTY-SIX

H uggins was small and swift and he seemed to know exactly where he was going. He didn't head for the Twisted Gates, as Milly expected. Instead he threaded through the trees. It wasn't long before Milly heard Charlie's yell of triumph, off to her right. *Great, they've caught the other twin,* she thought. A moment later, the air was filled with Gruffles' joyful barks and Wolfie's ecstatic perps.

Huggins showed no sign of having noticed. He pelted past the playing field and carried on going, towards the Wilderness. Milly had never been this far before. As far as she knew no one had, because it was common wisdom around Blaggard's that there was nothing beyond the playing fields worth bothering about.

The Wilderness was one of the few areas of Blaggard's that hadn't inspired any school myths. No one was supposed to have died there, or buried someone there, or even found any loot there, stolen, stashed and subsequently forgotten by some long-dead Blaggardian.

Still a little befuddled by the effects of the knock out gas, Milly struggled to keep up. But she was determined. Her eyes never left Huggins' fleeing back. *He's not gonna get away. I owe Wolfie. And Gruffles,* she thought. *And apart from that, he tried to destroy the school and Ms Martinet.* Her anger spurred her to push herself harder, to run a bit faster.

The Wilderness was approached through an arched door, set into a high, crumbling brick wall that stretched without break to the left and right. A faded wooden sign on the door simply said: WELCOME. That would be sufficient to put off any Blaggardians looking for adventure, Milly thought. They never went anywhere they were supposed to go. It was a matter of pride.

Huggins didn't hesitate. He charged at the door, shoved it open and slipped through.

Milly was seconds behind him.

An unexpected world was revealed. A long time ago, the Wilderness would have been beautiful and perhaps, in a neglected way, it still was. The last roses of the year straggled over the walls in a mass of fading colour. Formal flowerbeds, so overgrown that it was impossible to distinguish where one plant ended and another began, were intersected by paths obscured by creeping weeds.

Statues were dotted around, so choked by encroaching ivy that it looked as if they were being devoured by man-eating plants. As she sped by, Milly had a brief impression of a thick-bodied man with a scowl and an ugly hat. *Sir Thomas Blaggard?* But there was no time to think about it.

Ahead of her, Huggins had jumped over a low wall and onto a – Milly wasn't exactly sure what Huggins was now standing on. A boarded-over pond? A swimming pool? It was the size of a tennis court and was surrounded by cracked paving stones. The whole area was covered by sheets of wood, nailed together. Huggins was moving around carefully, eyes down as if he was looking for something.

By now, Milly had reached the covered area. She put one foot onto it and tested its strength. It seemed solid. She stepped onto the wooden covering.

Huggins stopped, somewhere near the centre. He was breathing heavily, eyes boring into Milly's as she approached him.

'You can't escape, Ethereus. Or are you Cumulus?' she used names deliberately, hoping to throw him off guard. 'You ran the wrong way. You should've headed for the gates. Your brother's not around to help you pull one of your tricks.'

Huggins sneered. 'Believe me, I could have escaped if I'd wanted to, brother or no brother. I had something else in mind.'

'What? Getting revenge for your big sister? We caught Badpenny and we can catch you. There'll be so many Badpennys in prison, they'll have a build a special wing to hold you all.'

Huggins looked unconcerned. 'I don't think so. Yes, I'm a Badpenny. And proud of it. And yes, we're here – my brother Cumulus and me – to get revenge for what you did to Pecunia – you and your bumbling sidekick and that treacherous Wolf and Griselda Martinet. I suppose you know that the Brain is in the safe in our den but–'

'I didn't, but I do now.' Milly gave him a sarcastic smile, edging closer.

For a second, a look of vexation crossed over Huggins' face. He looked down again and with grim deliberation, began to inch backwards. Milly followed. She was almost within grabbing distance. *He's not that much bigger than me. I've got a good chance, especially after those Bring Down A Grown-Up sessions in Miss Grimbly's Killer Kung Fu Club,* she was thinking. She prepared to pounce.

'I really wish I'd had the chance to release the Mole onto the Dependable world,' Huggins taunted. 'I was looking forward to destroying all their famous buildings, and all the pathetic Dependables in them at the same time.' He looked sly. 'It was *wonderfully* painful for him, when we converted him. I knew he wasn't dormant. Not totally. He deserved the pain. Agony would be a better word for it –'

Milly had heard enough. She lunged. Huggins sidestepped, delicately, as if he was treading on thin ice. Milly stumbled forward. As she fell faded words, stencilled onto the wood, seemed to rise up to taunt her:

DANGER –
SEWAGE VIEWING AREA

THIS TRAPDOOR IS FRAGILE

So there IS a sewage container, she thought, fleetingly. Too late, she saw the rope loop that must open the trap door.

Automatically, her hands came out to break her fall. They went straight through the old wood, plunging into the darkness and into something cold and cloying and oily.

She closed her mind to what it probably was, and concentrated on survival. She pulled her hands out, dragging them over the fractured wood, ignoring the tearing pain as splinters pierced the tender skin of her wrists. She tensed her muscles to struggle around, but Huggins was on her, forcing her down again into the stinking blackness. Before her head ducked below the level of the covering, Milly had a brief glimpse of cracks appearing as the old wood began to split. Below her, and so close that her hair was trailing in it, was nothing but bubbling black filth.

With all her strength, Milly wriggled and fought her way up, twisting round so that she was glaring up into Huggins' face. A sudden thought leapt into her mind. With lightning speed, she grabbed the $\mathcal{E}$ button on her frock coat.

'Get off me,' she spat. 'If you don't, I'll press the Emergency button!'

That made Huggins hesitate. But not for long. 'Press it,' he spat back.

Milly gritted her teeth and pressed.

The effect wasn't quite as dramatic as she'd hoped. The enamel $\mathcal{E}$ pinged off and landed on the wood. It rolled away and dropped into the slime with a little plop. Milly waited. Huggins was waiting too, with gritted teeth.

And then a tinny voice began piping from the button: 'Welcome to Blaggard's Emergency Hotline. If you believe that Crumleians are on the premises, please say 1. If you don't know what to steal next, please say 2. If you find yourself tempted to tell the truth on a regular basis, please say 3...'

Milly raised her eyes to the heavens. *Typical of Blaggard's. Nothing is what you think it is. Or what it should be.* She ripped the button off her coat and threw it into the ooze. The tinny voice continued as the button sank: '...If you are having Dependable longings, please press...'

She glared at Huggins, who was gloating now.

'If I'm going in, you're going in with me,' she promised.

Huggins grasped her wrists, grimacing as he realised that they were smeared with the contents of the huge pool. 'I don't think so,' he spat at her, pushing her down again. 'You're going in and you'll stay in. There's no one here to get you out.'

'Spoken with an inaccuracy that is *ab-so-lutely* typical of a Badpenny,' a voice said, behind them.

Huggins craned around, gaping. Quickly, Milly rolled to one side, gasping for breath. Griselda Martinet had crept up on them with her usual catlike stealth.

Without hesitation she gave Huggins a sharp push. He stumbled backwards. Straight into the widening hole. Ms Martinet stepped back, wiping her hands. 'Odious little squirt,' she commented, without emotion.

Huggins went under, emerging a second later coated with unspeakable black slime. Gasping, he wiped it from his eyes and mouth.

'I'm coming back to get you,' he spluttered.

Ms Martinet tilted her head. 'I don't see how,' she said. 'And even if you do, we'll smell you coming.'

He sank again. And this time, he didn't reappear.

A little gingerly, as if she wasn't used to touching other human beings, Griselda Martinet grasped Milly by the arm and helped her to her feet.

They walked away without a backwards glance.

'Thanks, Miss,' Milly said.

'He must have shaved his monobrow to hide his true identity. All Badpennys have one, together with an inflated perception of their own brilliance,' Ms Martinet said, with her cold smile. 'Let's hope that's the last of them. There *can't* be any more! Can there?'

CHAPTER THIRTY-SEVEN

B y the time they got back, people were starting to come round from the effects of the knock-out gas. William Proctor got up, blinked around and said: 'I strongly suspect something of a criminal nature has occurred.'

His father glared at him. 'Really? You don't say.'

Milly's mum was already on her feet and was getting things organised. 'People who want to throw up, stagger into the back, please. Perhaps you could aim your expulsions into the boxes of plastic chickens, to save clearing up later... Who feels up to guarding Miss Vipond and Mr Babington and whichever Huggins this is, until Ms Martinet makes plans for them?'

A dozen hands shot in the air, including Herman Blight's. He seemed to be making sheep's eyes at Milly's mum. *Yuk!* Milly thought.

Arthur Dillane was still coming round. When he'd regained his senses he stretched out on the floor and let his wife get on with it. 'I learned long ago not to interfere,' he said to Milly. 'Your mother is an amazing woman.'

Charlie was kneeling in front of the buckled safe with a look of intense concentration on his face. He threw Milly a relieved smile when she walked back in.

'I knew you'd be OK,' he Fabricated. 'Where's Huggins or Badpenny or whatever you want to call him?'

Milly grimaced. 'I don't think he'll be bothering us any more. He's in deep – shloop. Ms Martinet pushed him in the real sewage container. It's in the Wilderness. Don't let Gruffles down there, will you? He'll be throwing himself in faster than a Badpenny can shave off his monobrow. *Where* are they, by the way – Gruffles and Wolfie, I mean?'

'Back in my room... Bet Gruffles'll find his way into that sewage pit at some point. That dog has a nose for trouble.' He frowned at the safe again. 'I'm trying to get this open. I thought maybe the Brain might be in there.'

Milly was about to tell him that it definitely was, but she thought better of it. *Let him discover it for himself. You don't always need to be the one who knows everything.*

'Could be. Definitely worth checking. Need a hand?'

Charlie shook his head. 'No. No, I want to do it myself... aha!'

He pulled the door open and peered inside. 'I thought so!' He took out a black velvet cushion. Nestling on it was a lumpy diamond on a gold chain. It was the size of a walnut and it bore a distinct resemblance to a miniature brain. Even in the muted light of the Sewage Room, it glinted in a way that was almost hypnotic.

'Ms Martinet'll be over the moon.' He caught the Head

Teacher's eye, held up the chain and gave her a big grin. She raised her eyebrows and prowled over.

'Brilliant,' Milly said, as the Head Teacher was approaching. 'You've opened your very first old-fashioned safe without destroying it. And you've saved Blaggard's and Ms Martinet.'

Charlie gave a proud grin. 'As long as the school inspection goes well,' he said. 'That's if Dr X ever turns up–'

'Actually, Dr X has already turned up,' a voice behind them said.

They spun around. Mr Hobbes was standing behind them. Somehow he didn't look so helpless any more. There was a glint of sharp intelligence in his blue eyes. He shook Ms Martinet's hand.

'Perhaps it's time I introduced myself properly. My name *is* Hobbes. Doctor Xerxes Hobbes, at your service.'

For once, Ms Martinet seemed to be at a loss for words. She opened her mouth. Shut it. Tried again. 'I'll go and start packing my bags, then,' she said, in a flat voice. 'This day has been nothing short of–'

'– a triumph!' Dr X exclaimed. 'Pure anarchy. Exactly what a good criminal school needs to be. How else can young felons learn to think on their feet? They need to be prepared for whatever gets thrown at them. I can think of no better proving ground than Blaggard's. My congratulations, Ms Martinet!'

The Head Teacher was speechless. But not for long. Soon she was smiling and accepting Dr X's compliments as if the day had unfolded just as she'd planned it.

Leaving her basking in Dr X's praise like a cat in a shaft of sunshine, Milly and Charlie wandered outside.

'Everything OK, then?' Milly asked.

'Yep. Another threat dealt with. Dunno how Blaggard's ever managed without us,' Charlie said. He bent down, picked up a stick and threw it into the distance.

'Between us, I mean,' Milly persevered, looking up into his face. 'There's been times recently when we haven't got on very well. I know I can be a bit – bossy sometimes. And I thought maybe I was getting on your nerves. So–'

Charlie held up a hand. 'Stop. It's cool. You're cool. We're cool. It was Agatha. Telling me I'd be better off without you. I *knew* she was wrong, of course. But, you know –' he shrugged.

Milly's eyebrows rose into her fringe. 'I bet she was jealous. We're a team. A pretty amazing team. You do the hacking and electronics and robot dog wrangling–'

'–and you do the planning and working stuff out and saying cutting things to enemies!' Charlie finished for her. 'What's next, I wonder? Giant man-eating bats? *More* Badpennys? Something even worse?'

'Who knows?' Milly grinned up at him. 'Whatever it is, we'll sort it out. Between us.'

She gave him a friendly punch on the arm. Together they turned back to the chaos that was Blaggard's School for Tomorrow's Tyrants – their home.